LEO

A NAVY SEAL VETERAN ROMANCE

LISA CARLISLE

LISACARLISLEBOOKS.COM

Leo

Created with Vellum

❦ Created with Vellum

For E. Always.

ABOUT LEO

By Lisa Carlisle

A Beauty and the Beast-inspired Navy SEAL romance!

Leo: I hide in my Vermont cottage so nobody can see me.
I've seen the stares. I read their contemplation in their inquisitive expressions-how did I get those scars?

I refuse to spend the holidays with my parents as I'll bring everyone down. Worried about me, they send a caretaker. That's not going to happen. I'll turn her away at my front door.

When Rosanna arrives, she's not the matron I expect. She's young, pretty and curvy. And she comes with food to prepare dinner.

Hmm, it's been a long time since I had a home-cooked meal. Maybe I can tolerate her here for just one night.

Rosanna: I'll do anything to avoid spending another Christmas with my stepfamily and this temporary job gives me an excuse.

When I arrive at the remote stone cottage in the woods, I'm

stopped by a man with a scarred face and deep scowl. Leo turns me away. He didn't agree to this arrangement.

I don't have a backup plan. What am I going to do?

Fortunately, the groceries I brought to prepare dinner buy me some time. Leo agrees to let me cook for him (how generous) and to stay for one night.

Only we're hit with more snow than expected, and I'm stuck there if I don't want to freeze to death.

Leo will let me stay on one condition-never enter his studio.

CHAPTER 1

ROSANNA

"What do you mean you're not coming home for winter break?" my father asked. His voice grew so loud I had to pull the phone away from my ear.

I winced. Even though I'd planned on telling him about this, the shock in his voice tugged at my heart strings and left me feeling guilty.

"Dad, I found a job over holiday break. It pays well and will make it easier for me to finish my last semester. I can't pass up this opportunity."

Since the café I'd worked at had just closed down, I had to make money during break somehow. College was expensive. College in Boston, when you didn't have a full-time job, was even more so. My father didn't help with my finances. He couldn't with the way my stepmother and stepsisters burned through every dollar he earned, so I was on my own.

"But it's Christmas," he said in a wistful tone. "You have to come home for the holidays. It's a time when you should be with family."

I cringed. Maybe that was his family, but they'd never treated me as one of them. This job opportunity gave me an escape, so I *wouldn't* have to be with them. I didn't know what my father saw in Evelyn, his second wife. She was attractive and took care of herself, but that was what irked me—she only seemed to care about appearances. If he wanted to find someone who was the exact opposite of my mother, he succeeded. And Evelyn's two daughters were just like her. They lived for shopping and reality TV; two things I didn't care about. Whenever they brought up those topics, they teased me about my lack of knowledge. They looked down at their lowly, younger stepsister as if not knowing those things made me uncultured.

"Who would choose books over the real world?" They'd mock my love of reading. Since I had a book with me at all times, they had plenty of opportunities to glance down at my choice of paperback or my e-reader with disdain. As for my choice of studying for a master's in creative writing, that provided endless fodder for additional mockery. *"You'll never make any money writing. You're wasting your time on something that won't get you anywhere but tired and broke."*

Maybe so, but I'd rather take that route than the one they followed. They called themselves "influencers," although I think you had to have a decent-sized audience to make that claim. The last time I'd checked their social media profiles, they hadn't had much of a following.

I'd do anything to avoid spending the holidays with my step-family. That's why I had to convince my dad to let it go.

"Dad, it's only one Christmas. I can't pass up this chance. My sublet is ending."

"You can stay here."

A month with my stepsisters? Eek, no. "And I need a job. Not only did I find one, but I'll be in a cottage in Vermont where I'll have time to figure out what I want to write for my project."

I needed to write a novel or collection of short stories to graduate. Daunting. Although I'd known that requirement since I had enrolled, it now loomed over me. I'd written short stories and longer papers, but an entire *book*?

Maybe it was easier to go and deal with my stepfamily after all.

No, that was just fear talking.

"You can figure out what you want to do here," he countered.

Amid all the chaos and drama that surrounded my stepsisters, I wouldn't be able to accomplish that without earplugs. "I'll call on Christmas morning. You'll see my face, and it will be just like we're in the room together."

He snorted. "Not exactly."

Time for me to pull out my last excuse. It was one I hated to use, but absolutely true, and he knew it. "You know I don't feel like celebrating Christmas much anymore."

Not without my mom. That was her favorite holiday. She loved Christmas and would spend the weeks before it listening to holiday music while she baked and decorated. Without her exuberance, the festivities had never been the same.

"I know, Rosie." His voice softened.

I maneuvered the way to the end of the call. He wasn't happy about my decision but didn't try to talk me out of it again. After I ended the call, I pumped my fist in the air. Yes! I could avoid my stepfamily's constant reminders of how strange I was. I didn't fit into their world and didn't want to.

I finalized arrangements over the next week and moved my stuff to my friend Daniel's apartment. He had enough room in the basement to store my belongings until next semester. Then it was time to trek to Vermont.

A family had hired me as a caretaker for their son, Leo. He'd been injured in the military and had spent the last six months living alone in their cottage in the mountains. They'd wanted him to come home for the holidays, but he'd refused.

I could relate to that. But his mother had sounded perfectly nice, and nothing like my stepmother. This woman sounded like she worried about her son. That's why she hired me to make sure he ate, had fresh air, and so on. It sounded like something a caring mom would do. Like what my mom would have done.

There was a downside. Of course, there had to be. His mother warned that he could be irritable. He couldn't be worse than my stepmother and stepsisters, though, right? I envisioned an older guy who'd bark at me about my cooking or some other minor transgression. Maybe his parents were exaggerating, and he wasn't so bad. After all, families could be your staunchest supporters—or your harshest critics.

I pictured a quaint, cozy cabin. It might be kind of strange staying there with the grumpy stranger, but I'd deal with it.

Aside from making sure he ate healthy meals and took care of himself with basic hygiene, as well as taking care of the house, I was free to do what I wanted. I'd have plenty of time to sketch out ideas for my novel. If I was lucky and inspired, I might even start writing it.

My trek started with a bus from Boston. It was a slow crawl north through segments of high traffic. At least it wasn't the Christmas eve pandemonium, which we'd have next week. Once in Vermont, the traffic died down, but one slow driver on the single-lane road held everyone up. I ignored the grumbling from other passengers on the bus to focus on the rolling hills and snow-covered caps of the Green Mountains. What a magical landscape; so different from the tall buildings and concrete in the city.

The skies grew darker as we continued, an indication of the impending snowstorm tonight. Four to eight inches of snow were expected. I'd chosen to arrive before the storm rather than being slowed down by the cleanup afterward. Unfortunately, the darkness cast an ominous mood for the journey. I tried to brush it off as trepidation in venturing into the unknown, but it still weighed on me.

When we arrived at the bus station, I stored my bags in a locker and then walked over to a nearby market. Since I didn't know if the cottage was stocked with food, I used the food allowance provided to pick up ingredients for a few meals and staples. Once I had two bags full of groceries, I grabbed a taxi, picked up my bags, and continued to Leo's house.

We drove away from the bus station and down residential roads. The longer we drove, the more land separated each house. Soon there were more trees than signs of people.

We turned onto a narrow dirt road that had some snow patches and then continued on a long winding stretch uphill. As we left signs of civilization, my heart beat faster. I attempted to shake off a prickly sensation as just nerves.

The driver pulled up to a house with two levels covered in gray stone that stood on an empty patch of land surrounded by snow-covered evergreens. English ivy crawled up the stone and crept around the second-floor windows. Smoke drifted out of the stone chimney and disappeared in wisps into the cloudy gray sky.

This was the cottage? It was more like a castle in the middle of the forest.

I swallowed. Why did the tall gray walls seem imposing? Was it because the house was much larger than I expected?

A sense of foreboding gripped me. I'd be alone out here with a stranger. Perhaps I'd been gullible to be lured here by the promise of the well-paying job.

No. I gripped the door handle. My anxiety was the effect of watching too many horror movies. I suppressed the urge to tell the driver I'd changed my mind.

Instead, I said, "Thanks," and forced myself to climb out of the car.

The view of the snow-covered mountains in the distance was incredible, even muted by the hovering fog. The scent of pine trees and freshly fallen snow was a refreshing change from the smog of living in the city. I gathered my bags and stared up at the house ahead.

The driver turned the car around, kicking up snow, and left. A gust of wind rustled through the trees, and snow cascaded off branches. I should have asked him to wait. After all, I might have the wrong address or Leo might not be home or… I swallowed. A light was on, so he must be home. It must be my nerves kicking up again.

I hunched, bracing against the cold air that bit at my exposed skin. Living in a remote house during a Vermont winter might have seemed more magical in fantasy than reality. New England winters could be harsh.

I bit my lip and then groaned. Holidays with my stepfamily were harsher.

After taking a deep breath, I pushed myself toward the front door that was flanked on either side with stone columns. This was an opportunity. I was just scared of the unknown. I wouldn't run away without knowing what was on the other side of those doors.

LEO

I didn't need anyone taking care of me, let alone some stranger invading my private space.

I'd come to my family's cottage to isolate myself and was making it my own space. They hadn't come here for at least five years before I did, and it had shown signs of abandonment. They said I could live there if I fixed it up. That's how I'd been spending my time since the summer, and I had no plans to leave. Besides, nobody should have to spend the season with a brooding grump like me, especially during the holidays.

Just because they still owned the house didn't mean they could control my living situation. Why would they hire someone to come to the cottage and babysit me like I was a child? I was almost thirty years old, damn it. Although, sometimes I felt at least twice that age.

That was courtesy of being in the military for a decade and seeing too much as a Navy SEAL. Gone were the days of me being a gung-ho teen who thought he could make a difference in the world. Had I accomplished a damn thing in the end? Debatable.

The woman would be arriving soon. I pictured a matronly type who was around my mother's age, ordering me to eat my vegetables. What kind of bullshit was that? I cooked for myself and kept my place clean. Hell, I knew how to survive living in the wilderness.

Had my mother warned this caretaker about my scars? Brutal slashes marred the left side of my face. Whenever someone saw me for the first time, they tried not to stare, but I knew. They saw and they speculated about what happened.

I didn't even know myself. I remembered the blast and then nothing. When I woke in the hospital with souvenir gashes on my body, I couldn't remember what had happened.

Then I learned the news—two SEAL buddies on my team weren't as lucky as me.

Or maybe they were—they didn't have to live with the aftermath. The torment, the nightmares, the survivors' guilt. I was only feet away from them. How could such a short distance between us leave us with such different fates? Were all of our lives decided by chance? Or was it all predestined? Answers I'd never know.

I walked over to the mirror in the bathroom, the only one I tolerated on the main floor, and stared at the hideous scars. Once upon a time, women called me hot. Not anymore. What a cruel joke. I couldn't even smile without looking like a freak since the scar stretching to my mouth curled with distortion.

It wasn't as if I had anything to smile about, anyway. I closed myself off, away from the world, living like a hermit. If I stayed here alone, no one would be forced to endure my ugliness, both inside and out.

I was happier on my own.

Maybe not *happy*, but existing.

I found solace in the solitude. Alone in the forest, I didn't have to deal with anyone. I went for long hikes and breathed in the clean mountain air. When autumn arrived, I embraced the changing of the seasons and the magnificent colors of the forest. The brilliant fall foliage was something I'd missed during my time away from Vermont. Winter was almost here, and we'd already had snowfall this month. Patches of snow remained on the ground. With the snowfall expected overnight, I should be able to go cross-country skiing tomorrow.

My parents had wanted me to come home for the holidays. They lived a couple of hours away over the New York border, near Lake George. They didn't know what they were asking. If I walked into a party, my scowl would bring down any festive vibes.

I had nothing to celebrate this year.

While in the military, I'd looked forward to any holidays I could spend at home with family. It didn't always happen. When it did, I cherished it. But that was before the incident.

I'd spent the last ten years of my life as a SEAL, and now I wasn't one. I was an average schlub with no prospects, no future, and nothing to look forward to. I was plagued by nightmares about an incident I didn't even remember. The question that sounded in my mind every morning was *what now?*

All I had was military experience accompanied by trauma on both mind and body. I was nothing anymore. No one.

And nobody would want to be around me and my negativity, so it was best that I stayed here. Alone.

For my parents to send someone to look out for me wasn't acceptable. When I relayed this to my mother, she said it was too late, and it was already arranged. It wasn't healthy for me to be by myself, especially during the holidays. She'd hired someone, and the caretaker was on the way.

Wonderful. The trip would be a waste of time. As soon as the woman arrived, I'd tell her there was a mistake because I didn't agree to having someone live in the cottage with me, and she needed to leave. Sure, I might feel slightly bad about her trekking all this way, but we all faced tough lessons we had to swallow. The sooner she learned that, the less likely she'd expect anything from anyone. Because when it came down to it, we were all alone in the end.

At the sound of a car approaching, I walked over to the window. A dark blue SUV navigated down the dirt road. A woman climbed out of the back seat. I couldn't see her face as she was concealed by much of the car. She appeared to be pulling things from the backseat. How many bags was she bringing?

After the driver pulled away, I had a better view of the woman. She was younger than I expected—maybe early twenties. Her hair was long and brown, tucked under that black hat and cascading in waves over a button-down, yellow peacoat. She had wide, innocent eyes and a heart-shaped face. Pretty.

Not what I'd been expecting.

It didn't change anything. I didn't want her here. She had to leave.

She had a carry-on suitcase, backpack, and two large grocery bags. After struggling to lift them all, she abandoned her luggage on the stone path to carry the groceries first.

She headed to my front door.

I should have run out and stopped the driver before he drove off. My hesitation cost me. Damn curiosity. I could have asked him to stick around while I explained the situation to her. Then she'd climb her pretty little self back into the car, be on her way and out of my life.

Now, I had to deal with this young woman struggling to carry bags. A gentleman would rush out and help her.

I wasn't a gentleman. Not any longer.

I was a beast.

CHAPTER 2

ROSANNA

ere goes. I dropped the grocery bags in front of the red door, which appeared more like a warning than a welcome. I then claimed my carry-on luggage and backpack. Raising my wavering hand, I lifted the lion-head brass knocker and rapped on the door. It sounded much louder than the light, friendly knock I'd planned.

The door flew open, and I gasped, taking a step back.

A man stood in the doorway, staring at me with a grim expression. He was tall, towering over me by around a foot, and muscular—that was noticeable even through his black sweater. He was younger than I expected, maybe in his late twenties, with dark hair and arresting blue eyes.

A long scar stretched down one side of his face, crisscrossing a smaller one that curved toward his mouth. An instant pang of empathy rose within. I knew he was a Navy SEAL who had been injured and could only guess that his scars were connected to a brutal experience.

He didn't fit what I'd pictured, save for the surly expression. He stepped outside and closed the door behind him.

"What are you gasping about?" he barked. "My scars?"

What a way to make my entrance—drawing attention to his wound. "N-no," I stammered. "You opened the door so quickly. I—I—uh, wasn't expecting such a quick response."

His mouth twisted with disdain. "I don't have time for screwing around."

So much for a warm welcome. He didn't even invite me in but joined me outside. What was that about?

"I'm Rosanna Carreiro." I gave him a pleasant smile. "Your family sent me here."

He scowled and turned away. "Against my wishes." He exhaled from his nostrils with a whoosh. "I've taken care of myself for the past ten years. I don't need a caretaker now." He patted his scarred cheek. "Look, I even remembered to shave," he added with sarcasm.

Okay then. I'd been warned that he wouldn't be friendly but wasn't prepared for such a curt welcome.

That was all right. I wouldn't be scared off so easily. I rubbed my arm. "Why don't we go inside to chat?" Plus, we'd be able to get out of the cold. The mountain air had a clean, refreshing scent, yet also the cool bite of the impending storm. I had a coat, hat, and gloves on, but he didn't. Although he wore a dark gray sweater, jeans, and black loafer-like slippers, I doubted they were warm enough to ward off the chill.

He arched his brows and scoffed, "Chat? What do you think this is, high school? I don't chat."

I sighed. Sure, I'd expected some pushback, but I hadn't even made it across the threshold.

"I'm sorry you came all this way, but as you can see, I don't need your services. Why don't you call for your driver to return? I'll be happy to pay for your trip from wherever you came and your earnings for the next two weeks to make up for the inconvenience."

Frustration added to the weight of my heavy backpack with my laptop and books. I removed the pack and put it beside the other bags. "I didn't come all this way just to turn around at your front door, Mr. Ricci."

"Mr. Ricci?" he repeated with a smirk. "No need for the formalities. It's Leo."

"Okay, Leo." I planted one hand on my hip. Travel irritation combined with this rudeness cut on my nerves. "I see you're not crazy about me being here, but you didn't hire me. I made an agreement with your parents. To fulfill my promise to them, I'd at least like to make sure you're doing okay. See if you need anything. Note if the property needs any upkeep."

"It doesn't. I have everything under control."

"Since it was a long bus ride here, I'm not thrilled about turning right back around to head back home, especially with the storm coming in tonight. Why don't you invite me in out of the cold so I can at least put this food away that I bought? I can then make us a cup of tea or cocoa or whatever you'd like to drink. If you don't want to talk, fine. But I'm not leaving until I at least fulfill my obligation to your parents to see that you're well and everything here is okay."

Leo gaped at me for several seconds. His lips twitched into a hint of a smile, which reached up to his eyes, making them twinkle. Without that broody expression, he looked handsome despite the scars. He must be self-conscious about them to point them out upon meeting me.

He barked out with a quick laugh. "You're a tough one in that little package, aren't you?"

Little? I might be short at five foot three inches, but with my ample curves, I wouldn't describe myself as little.

I exhaled and stared back at him. "Only when I'm pushed and need to be."

He raised his chin a notch and assessed me for a few seconds. "You made your point about what you said you'd do, and I respect that." He opened the door and stepped aside. "Besides, I don't like to see food going to waste." He motioned for me to enter and bent forward in a mock bow. "Welcome to my humble abode, Ms. Carreiro."

I shot him a look at his sardonic hospitality. "Thank you for the warm welcome," I returned, my tone matching his.

Then I lifted a couple of bags and entered the cottage. The shift from the cool breeze outdoors to the warmth of the cottage was abrupt, and I shuddered. The open living space was large yet cozy, complete with a fire burning in the fireplace. The stone design from the exterior carried indoors around the fireplace. The walls were dark paneled and covered with paintings of the forests and mountains.

A bookshelf caught my attention, as they often did. When I had a chance, I'd scour the titles. I pictured how nice it would be reading on the chocolate-brown, velvet sofa that was in front of the fireplace while the snow descended onto the trees outside the picture window.

An oval polished wood dining room table with six chairs seemed better suited for a family than a man who lived alone. The kitchen had modern fixtures and appliances that seamlessly blended into the old country style of the rest of the house.

The sharp sound of the shutting door startled me, and I sucked in a breath before spinning around. Leo had carried the remaining bags in and placed them down on the hardwood floor.

The stark realization that I'd pushed myself to enter this cabin with a man who didn't want me here hit me like a gust of wind from outside. Perhaps I'd been hasty in my pushiness to enter. The safer option might have been to bail as soon as I had a taste of his bitter personality. I could have told his parents I'd tried, but he wouldn't let me in.

Now I was alone with him in this massive cottage, away from everything and everyone. I gulped.

He glared at me and snorted. "Are you always so jumpy?"

LEO

Rosanna wasn't just pretty, she had spunk. I'd give her that. Most people would have scurried off because of the way I'd treated them. She stood her ground despite staring up at me from her petite stature on my doorstep, while I fought the urge to invite her in to protect her from the cold.

Then at the same time, she'd gasped like a heroine in a Gothic novel. The incongruence was amusing. Maybe we could have this little chat she proposed before I sent her on her way. After all, it wasn't as if I had any big plans tonight.

Or any night.

She glanced around the main level, her eyes widening as she circled halfway.

"As you can see, I haven't been living like a slob. When you've been in the military for a decade, you know how to keep a place clean."

"True. You've kept it tidy." She removed her gloves and then her black hat. Her dark, glossy hair was tousled by the movement.

My fingers itched with the sudden urge to touch it and see if it was as soft and smooth as it looked. Where the hell did that come from? She'd think I was some kind of sick freak. I pressed my fingers into my palm to stop myself from acting on a terrible impulse.

She caught my gaze. "I'll bring the food into the kitchen. Is it okay to put it away?"

I attempted to peek into the bags. "Depends on what you have there." What the hell? Why did that sound like flirting? I sure the hell wasn't. I didn't want her here in my space.

"Well, I bought ingredients to make lasagna for dinner tonight, as well as a salad and garlic bread."

Lasagna. My mouth watered at the idea of a rich, hearty meal—one of my favorites.

She peered down into the bags. "I also picked up some staples, like soups and pastas, in case the storm kept us from heading to the store."

The way she spoke about *us* being in the cottage together was cute but laughable. Did she really believe I was going to let some stranger live here and take care of me? I'd already gone to the store yesterday and stocked up on milk, bread, peanut butter, bananas, and apples. As for staples, I'd taken care of that during the first few days I'd moved in. I was a Navy SEAL. Of course, I'd be prepared. We had enough canned goods and water to get by for months.

"Go for it." I motioned for her to have her way in the kitchen, curious to see what she'd do.

Rosanna walked by me and put the shopping bags on the counter. She then removed her sunny yellow peacoat, and when she did, her pink sweater stretched over her breasts. My gaze roamed over the rest of her body with those mouth-watering curves. When she turned to fill the yellow kettle on the stove with water, my gaze lowered. Her ass was full and unquestionably luscious.

Rosanna turned over her shoulder. "Tea, coffee, or cocoa? What's your poison?"

I tore my gaze from her ass but not before she must have caught me staring. My mouth twitched into a grin before I squashed it. She was intriguing. Didn't she feel any fear about being alone here with me, a stranger? Not only that, but someone so cantankerous and unwelcoming, and who ogled her curves?

Ah hell, it had been too long since I'd been with a woman. I

hadn't since before the incident. But back th
scarred. Who would want me now?

Definitely not a woman who was paid t
care of my ass, so I better get my head out

After all, she did have a trek here. I con
and not let her have a warm beverage befor_
way. "I'm all set but help yourself." I gestured toward the kit_

I walked over to sit on my black leather recliner in the living room. Then I picked up a DIY magazine for home projects, pretending to be not at all interested in what she was doing.

I peeked up to watch her empty the shopping bags onto the counter and then put food away.

She opened the fridge. "Oh good. You have plenty of food here."

"Right." I smirked. "I know how to go food shopping."

She'd almost finished putting everything away when the kettle sounded. She brewed a mug of tea. A few minutes later, she removed the tea bag and came to sit on the sofa near where I was on the recliner.

She sipped her tea and then cradled her mug in both hands. "What do you do to keep yourself busy out here?"

I arched a brow. "Why are you asking? So you can report back to my parents?"

"They worry about you."

"I'm well aware." I exhaled. "My mom reminds me all too often. Every time she hears about a veteran's suicide, she calls to check on me with panic in her voice."

Rosanna winced. She attempted to cover it up by raising the mug to her lips and taking another sip.

"Does that bother you?" I asked.

"Doesn't it bother everyone?" she replied.

"No idea." I shrugged. "I don't know what civilians think about. Do they even know we exist?"

course." Rosanna studied me for several seconds. "Your
ts care about you. Otherwise, I wouldn't be here."

"You don't *need* to be here," I reminded her. I motioned to the
kitchen. "I've stocked up on food. I'm not going to starve out
here in the wilderness." I placed a hand on my chest. "Here in
the Vermont woods, I'm far away from the danger I'd faced in
other parts of the world. My mother worried enough then. She
doesn't need to now."

Rosanna tipped her head. "Can you blame her? She's your
mother. She'll probably never stop worrying about you."

I grunted. "Does your mother still worry about you?"

Rosanna lowered her gaze to the maroon oriental rug. "My
mother's dead."

Fuck. I was such an ass. Although she'd said it in a flat voice,
I heard the pain. I swallowed, wishing I could bite back my
stupid words. "I'm sorry. I didn't know."

"There's no way you would have." Her voice sounded flat, as
if she'd explained this many times.

At least she didn't fix a hateful, accusatory stare on me. Wait,
why would I care? I didn't know her. I didn't care a whiff about
what she thought of me.

Still, I wasn't a complete monster.

Although the immediate question that followed was to ask
what happened, I couldn't be callous and voice it. If she wanted
to tell me, that was her choice.

I adjusted my position in the recliner. "You can assure my
mother that I'm not a risk to myself or anyone around me."

"I'm sure she'll be relieved to hear that." Rosanna's brows
edged up a fraction. "If I was in her shoes and had a child
serving in dangerous locations, I'm sure I'd be a wreck."
Rosanna grimaced. She took another sip of tea and glanced into
the kitchen. "The meat and sausage I brought for the lasagna is
in the fridge. You should use it soon or put it in the freezer." She

bit her lower lip. "Or I'm happy to stay and cook it, as I'd planned, before I leave."

She did go to all that trouble to shop for me and planned to cook dinner for tonight. Did I have to kick her out right away? It was lasagna after all. Sure, I could make it myself, but there was something nice about someone cooking comfort food for you.

Could I stomach sitting through a meal with her? That way, she could go back and tell my parents she made sure I was well fed. Even if I didn't want her around, one dinner wouldn't kill me. I'd been though a whole hell of a lot worse.

Besides, she could use a nice meal before a bus ride, even if she was preparing it herself.

"You went out of your way to lug those groceries here," I told Rosanna. "And I hate wasting food. So, we might as well cook it up and eat it."

CHAPTER 3

LEO

"Sure," Rosanna agreed and then pulled out her phone. "Let me look for the next bus, first." She groaned. "Oh no."

"What?"

"The next one to Boston is tomorrow afternoon."

My heart jolted. "What?" I wasn't getting stuck with her all night. No way. "That can't be right. Let me see." After she handed me her phone, I saw that it was indeed correct. "Surely, there are other options."

"I looked into them already. That's the quickest and easiest," she added. "Don't worry. I can book a hotel near the bus station tonight."

I heaved a sigh of relief. "I'll pay for it and for the ride there."

"Thanks." She sighed. "I'm relieved it's not right away." She groaned. "The last thing I want to do after a long bus ride is turn back for another long bus ride."

My jaw clenched. Nobody would want that. But this wasn't

my doing. She wasn't my problem. "Okay." I could tolerate a few more hours with this stranger before returning to my quiet life.

There was also the storm later tonight. I couldn't put her at risk so I would make sure she was at the hotel by then.

While Rosanna cooked in the kitchen, I connected my phone to a speaker in the living room area. I played a podcast that alternated between music I liked and news updates. I grabbed my laptop from the coffee table and sat in my recliner. Then I scrolled through my feeds.

Soon, the scent of tomato sauce with spices reached me. I had to admit, it smelled good.

"If you're trying to work your way into a man's heart, it's not going to work." I gritted my teeth.

She turned and raised a spoon covered in sauce. "I'm here to work, not win anyone's heart."

"Easy, tiger." I motioned, lowering my hand. "It was a joke. A bad one." Although her reaction had amused me.

Nobody was working their way into my heart, especially not now. It happened once, and it hadn't worked out. That was when I was young and whole. Now I was damaged and scarred, even less appealing. It was better that I kept people at a distance. That way, they couldn't reject me.

I tried to busy myself with the nonsense on my screen, but often stole glances at her. How could I not with her right there in my kitchen?

I swallowed. My interest was only because I hadn't been with a woman in a long time.

Every sound from the kitchen gave me an excuse to peek. After a few minutes, I realized that ignoring a beautiful, curvy woman who was fiddling about in the cottage was impossible. I gave up on trying to distract myself and closed my laptop.

I walked into the kitchen. "What can I do?"

"You don't have to do anything." She turned to me with

surprise. Her hair fell over one eye, and she brushed it back. "One of the things I was hired to do is cook."

Right. She was only here to do a job. She had zero desire to be with me in particular. So, I better not look at those curves and think about them again.

"I can't just sit here and watch you make a mess," I barked while gesturing to the counters. That part was true. Everything smelled good, but the kitchen was a disaster. Chopping boards with vegetables in various states spread across the counter amid pans and dishes.

She glanced around. "I know I make a mess when I cook, but don't worry, I'll clean it all up."

"And like I said, I'm fully capable of preparing a meal. Tell me what needs to be done, and I'll do it."

Why I couldn't have offered to help in a kinder way was something I wouldn't understand. Did I have to be so gruff?

Despite my harsh tone, she didn't flinch. "Fine. You can prep the salad." She pointed to the bags of vegetables near the sink. "Just make sure you wash everything first."

"Yes, ma'am." I straightened, amused at her bossy tone.

Although we got in each other's way a few times, it didn't bother me. That's how it had been when I spent time here with my family growing up. The house was always bustling with activity. My sister and I would usually have a friend or two come visit for a week or so during summer breaks.

Having Rosanna here reminded me of the times when there was life in this cabin. It was kind of nice to work on a meal here with someone. Preparing meals alone, and only for me, had been my way for months. Where was the pleasure in that?

By the time we sat at the table in the dining room area, I was starving. Everything smelled so good, I could dive in and shovel forkfuls into my mouth. Maybe I would have if I were alone. But I wasn't, and I'd try to remember my manners at the dinner table.

We each had a plate with lasagna and a bowl of salad. I smirked, proud at my little contribution that showed her, *see, I can feed myself.*

A loaf of warmed garlic bread sat in a basket between us. We reached for a slice at the same time, and our fingers brushed.

I pulled my hand away as if I'd touched a hot stove. Heat lingered on my fingertips as if that was indeed the case. Avoiding eye contact, I took a bite of the lasagna. The flavorful sauce and cheese danced on my tongue. Then I bit into the meat. Delicious and juicy. Everything was damn good.

"This isn't bad," I said. "Where did you get the recipe for the sauce?"

"Old family secret," she replied with a sly grin. "Just kidding. The internet."

"Ahh, the source of all information." I gave her a sage nod.

I took another forkful of lasagna and almost moaned. Letting her stay for dinner wasn't a bad idea. At least I had a hearty meal out of it.

"How do you spend your time?" I asked, curious about this woman in my cottage.

"I'm in grad school in Boston."

"What are you studying?"

"Creative writing. I'm almost done with my MFA."

"You want to be a writer?"

"I do."

"What do you want to write about?"

Her gaze drifted off. "I'd love to write novels. No matter how lost or sad I was, I found a way to escape for a little while when reading a book. I could travel with another character into their world, go through their experiences with them. It made things seem… better. More tolerable." She grimaced. "But I need to write close to one-hundred pages of fiction as my final project this spring, and I'm not sure I can pull it off."

"Why not?"

She shook her head. "I don't know. The pressure, maybe? I try to think of ideas, but none of them are good enough."

"Maybe you're being too hard on yourself."

She shrugged. "Maybe." Glancing off into the distance, she added, "I was hoping to find inspiration while I was here."

I resisted a snort. That would have to hit as quick as lightning as she wouldn't be here for long. "Why would you come here for Christmas? Don't you have somewhere to go?"

She flinched and nudged her chin up. "I do. I typically spend it with my father and stepfamily."

I hit a sore spot. "Don't you want to go there?"

"Nope."

"Why not?"

She brought her fingertips together. "Oh, we're leaping right into the personal questions, are we?"

I rolled my shoulders. "I think I should know the background of a stranger who comes into my home," I barked.

"No need to get defensive." She tipped her head and exhaled. "The truth is I would rather not be with my stepfamily."

"Why not?" I groaned. "Or is that too personal as well?"

"I don't mind telling you. After all, you're right. I would want to know the same thing about someone hired to stay under my roof."

"What do you know about me?"

"I know what your family chose to tell me." She turned her hand up. "If it's the full story, I have no idea. Only you do."

"Why don't you tell me?"

"They told me that you were injured overseas, and it ended your military career. You chose to come here to recover but were alone. And we already covered how they were worried about you."

That was the basics of what happened. I left out specific details, all the nuances, and the toll that it took, ripping through my soul.

31

Without bothering to confirm or deny what she said, I turned the questions back on her. "You didn't answer my question. Why would you choose to be here over the holidays?"

She pressed her lips together. "Because I don't want to be with them. My stepmother and stepsisters are superficial. All they care about are appearances and fashion. They think I'm a freak for not being like them." She shuddered. "I'd hate to be like them." She exhaled with a low sigh. "My mother died when I was ten. My father remarried, and I never really hit it off with his new wife. She has two daughters, both older than me. He thought it would be great for me to have sisters. He was wrong. We might be close in age, but we have nothing in common. Might as well be a different species."

I felt for her. Being different or feeling alone. To lose her mother at a young age and then be forced to live with a family where she didn't fit in had to be hard. "How are you different?"

"If I'm going to answer your personal questions, you'll have to answer some of mine."

I snorted. "We'll see."

"About what?"

"It depends on your questions. Then I'll decide if I want to answer."

She stared at me. "Fair enough." She took a sip of wine and put the glass down. With her gaze fixed on the table, she said, "We have different interests. I like to read and write. Whenever they see me doing either, they scoff, telling me what a waste of time it is. They note there are far more interesting things in the world, like shopping and fashion and celebrity gossip. They laugh at my simple style, which they call basic."

My gaze lowered to her soft pink sweater, and I snatched it back up before I stared at her breasts.

"They say I hide from the world instead of experiencing it."

I grunted. Not even sure what to say.

She fixed her gaze on me. "Do you think like that?"

I snorted. "I think I'm the perfect example of hiding from the world."

She slanted her head. "Why do you do so?"

I clucked my tongue. *That* was getting too personal. Time to deflect. "What about your stepmother?"

"She's not as outright critical as my stepsisters are. But let's say it's not hard to figure out where they got their mindset from." Rosanna tapped her fingertips together, appearing to get agitated. "She's always trying to get me to dress better. Dropping hints about the gym or new diets or outright telling me I'd look so much better if I lost weight."

Rosanna was beautiful the way she was. I'd hate for her to lose those curves. I couldn't say that without sounding like a creep, though. That would be a sure-fire way to send her dashing for the door.

Wait, that's what I wanted. Right?

"What about your father?"

"I see we've moved on to the twenty questions portion of the dinner," she teased.

"Right on schedule." A smile tugged at my lips. When I realized I was smiling, I forced it away. I knew how twisted it made me look.

She told me about her father. He sounded laid back and let his wife call the shots. When I asked her about her mother, that's when Rosanna's expression faltered.

"She was wonderful. Beautiful and loving. I miss her every day."

She turned away, glancing around the room. "Need a refill?"

I sensed her need to avoid that discussion.

"No." I gestured at the plate. "Everything was delicious. I'm glad I agreed to this dinner."

"With some stubbornness," she teased.

I laughed, surprising myself. I enjoyed her spunk.

"All right, I think I answered enough in this interrogation." She motioned to me. "Your turn."

I groaned. Why did I agree to this? "What do you want to know?"

"Is what your family described to me true?"

I swallowed. "Essentially."

"That's it?"

"Yes."

She inclined her head and watched me.

I shifted in my chair. "That's the gist of the situation. Not the details, though."

"Would you like to tell me about those?"

"No, this isn't a shrink session. Besides, I don't want to talk about that to anyone."

She nodded. "Understandable." After a few seconds, she asked, "Have you ever written about it?"

I frowned and shook my head.

"Some veterans find writing about their experiences helpful. It's a cathartic way to deal with what they've gone through."

I grunted. "I'm not a writer."

"You don't have to be. You're not writing it for anyone else, just yourself." She placed her hand on her chest. "That's how I started writing. I started in middle school, writing in journals. I filled volume after volume. Of course, it was tons of angsty griping during puberty. But it helped to cope with the rough transition. Now when I look back and read those pages, I laugh. Things that were such a big deal at the time mean nothing now. Utterly forgettable."

My muscles hardened. I tried to relax the tension on the next exhale. "I wouldn't be able to forget what I went through."

She shuffled in her chair and flashed me a sheepish glance. "That's not what I mean. I'm not trying to dismiss what you went through." She ran her hand through her hair. "I guess I'm saying that when you put something that bothers you on paper, sometimes it loses the power it has over you. Getting it out of your head can be freeing in a way."

I cleared my throat. This conversation was tripping too close to over the line where I felt comfortable. "What works for one person doesn't necessarily work for another."

"True."

"Besides, I'm not going to talk about this to a stranger."

"Understandable." She glanced at my empty plate. "I should clean up and order a ride to the hotel."

I could offer to drive her. That would be what a gentleman did. I wasn't one. "Where are you going to go from there? Back to campus?"

"No. I was subletting, but that's over."

"To your stepfamily?" I'd feel like a real ass if I sent her right to where she was trying to avoid.

"No. I already told my father I'm not coming home." She huffed. "I'll figure something out."

A part of me felt badly for taking away this opportunity for her, but I didn't make the offer or agree to it. Like she said, she'd figure something out.

"What about a boyfriend?" The question came out strange, almost sounding jealous.

"I don't have one."

"I'm surprised."

"Why?"

"Look at you." I motioned to her. "You're young." And beautiful. I kept that part to myself.

She moaned. "After one too many awkward or downright disastrous dates, I'd decided to hold off on dating until after I graduate. That way, I can focus on finishing school and figuring out what I'm going to do next—without adding any more complications to my life."

With a grunt, I added, "Relationships are tricky."

"Oh." She cocked her head. "Are you saying this from experience?"

I ground my teeth. Should I tell her? I'd asked her personal questions. It was only right to reply. "Yes. I was serious with someone once, before I enlisted. What I quickly learned is that the military lifestyle isn't for everyone. She ended it soon after I enlisted." I shrugged. "My lifestyle wasn't compatible with a relationship."

I shouldn't have been surprised when Eva dumped me. She liked living a comfortable life, one that including spending my money. It wasn't mine, technically, but my family's. When my enlistment made it clear I wasn't going into my family's financial management business in upstate New York and would be stationed wherever the military decided, living on paychecks for a low-ranking enlistee, it was another wake-up call for Eva. I wasn't the right one for her. She ended our relationship and broke my heart.

"And now?" Rosanna asked.

I let out a mirthless laugh. "You're joking, right?"

"No."

She didn't appear to be teasing, so I answered. "I'm a mess. If I wasn't suitable to be in a relationship back then, I sure the hell am not now."

Discomfort roiled within me. Why did I bring this up? I pushed my chair back. "Dinner was good." It was delicious, but she didn't need to hear that. She might use that to push an argument to stay.

"I'll clean up the dishes."

When she walked into the kitchen, I watched her, but quickly snatched my gaze away. I shouldn't gawk at a woman I wanted out of my hair as soon as possible.

While we'd prepared and ate dinner, I hadn't noticed that it had started to snow. I turned on the local weather on the television. The snowstorm was starting sooner than expected—and we'd probably get more snow.

"Oh no," she muttered and stared at the TV. "I better get moving soon." She started to wash the dishes.

"Don't worry about that," I said. "Go ahead and order a ride. I can clean up."

"Thanks." She pulled out her phone and bit her lower lip. "The estimate is forty-five minutes."

That was cutting it close. I could drive her and then would end up driving back when the storm was picking up. That could be risky. Traveling *anywhere* during a snowstorm was. On the news, the forecast had changed. We weren't supposed to get the brunt of the snow storm originally, but it looked like its course had shifted. She shouldn't be traveling tonight, and neither should I.

"If it's as bad as they're saying it could be, the car may be canceled," I warned her.

"Hmmm..." Her face scrunched with a worried expression. "I'll figure something out." She tapped on her phone.

My skin tightened. I scratched my head. *Don't say it. You're not under any obligation to help her.*

"Just stay in the guest room for the night," I barked.

Rosanna blinked at me with a surprised expression.

"Oh, don't act like you weren't fishing for that invite."

She slowly slanted her gaze and arched one brow. "I wasn't."

Maybe not. Why was I doing this? I owed her nothing. She made a great dinner. So what? She was a big girl and could find her way home—wherever that was.

And if she ended up stranded somewhere in the snow on the side of the road...

I swallowed. That wouldn't be my fault. I didn't invite her here. Yet, I had delayed her departure by having her stay and cook for dinner. The temptation of home-cooked lasagna was too much to pass up, but now I was going to pay for it.

"If something happened to you, my mother would kill me," I justified.

Rosanna's eyes widened. "Are you sure you want me to stay?"

"I didn't say I *wanted* it," I snapped. "But it's the decent thing to do." I gestured toward the window. "No one wants to be stuck out there tonight." The gruffness returned to my voice. She must think I was a real beast. Still, she hadn't appeared scared of me yet, not at all.

"Okay." She stared at me for a few seconds and gave me a small smile. "Is one night with me such a sacrifice?"

I arched my brows.

Her cheeks turned pink, and she turned away. "You know what I mean—one night with me under your roof?"

I snorted. "Guess we'll find out." I stood. "I said you could stay for the night, didn't I? I wouldn't have invited you otherwise." I raised my index finger. "One night." I started up the upstairs. "Come with me. I'll show you the guest room."

That sentence sounded odd since I'd never called it that before. My sister hadn't come to the cottage for years, so there was no point keeping her room the way she'd had it set up. I'd converted her old room to be a guest room, figuring she'd claim it when she came to visit. I'd never had guests here, though. Then again, Rosanna wasn't a guest. More of a nuisance.

Okay, fine, a pretty nuisance.

Who could cook a delicious lasagna.

And was slightly entertaining with her sass, and a little cute when she blushed.

And had killer curves.

I rubbed the back of my neck. One night and she'd be out of my hair for good.

CHAPTER 4

ROSANNA

I woke to the sound of wind rustling my windows, jarring me with a reminder of where I was. The wind had howled through the forest during much of the night, leaving me wide-eyed and restless as I contemplated what was in the dark forest outside.

Yet, I must have fallen into a deep sleep eventually, cocooned by comfortable soft sheets. The dark wood, carved, four-poster bed was full of warm and cozy bedding. It was luxurious compared to the twin bed I'd gotten second hand, which was now in storage in a friend's basement.

Despite the coziness in this guest room with its pale-yellow walls and paintings of landscapes, coming here turned out to be a mistake. After all, Leo didn't want me here, and I got it. His mother had arranged this without him agreeing. I'd texted her yesterday to let her know I'd arrived. She'd replied to ask if there were any problems. Apparently, she knew her son. I hadn't replied yet with all the changes going on and said we were figuring things out. If me being here was going to be a point of contention between Leo and his mother, I didn't want to get involved. I was already inadvertently caught up in whatever this was—a battle of wills?

He was odd, though. He'd bark at me or scowl but then softened during dinner. He had incredible blue eyes—when they weren't staring at me with mistrust. His face was chiseled, and he had a strong jawline. He would have been considered conventionally handsome were it not for the scars that marred one side of his face. I didn't think they made him unattractive, though, especially when we talked.

He actually seemed interested in what I had to say. That was a rarity with many of the guys I'd met in college. They pretended to be listening before they made their move. That was one of the reasons I was done with dating in college. The guys I'd tried dating only wanted one thing. Maybe it was bad luck, or I attracted the immature and emotionally unavailable. Besides, I didn't need any distractions during this final semester, not with my project deadline looming ahead this spring.

Although I wanted to linger in the warm bed, I should figure out my next plan as soon as possible.

I texted my friend Daniel: *I made it to Vermont.*

He might not be up yet as it was still early.

Daniel: *Glad you're safe.*

Me: *You're up early.*

Daniel: *My family is loud.* He added a winking emoji. *How is it there?*

Me: *A little snafu—he doesn't want me here.*

Daniel: *What a jerk. So now what?*

Me: *I'm not sure yet. I'll get the bus back to Boston and see if anyone's around who I can crash with.*

Daniel: *You can come visit me in Jersey.*

Me: *Thanks, but I'm not going to intrude on your Christmas home with your family.*

Daniel: *No intrusion. They'd love to meet you.*

Me: *I'll keep that in mind. I'll let you know when I get back to Boston.*

I pulled down the comforter and climbed out of bed. I peeked outside. Sunlight drifted through the branches and snow blanketed the trees. It looked like well over a foot had fallen already, with more than two feet in areas with snow drifts. It was still snowing hard. I groaned. It wasn't going to be pleasant dealing with this.

I made the bed and got dressed. Might as well get this over with. I put on my snow gear and boots and went downstairs. I found a shovel outside where the breezy air had a bite. I started shoveling the snow off the steps. At least it was light and fluffy. It wasn't the wet, heavy stuff that could kill your back. As I continued down the path, the front door flew open.

"What are you doing?" Leo asked in a surprised tone.

I stopped to look at him. "Shoveling." I resumed scooping up snow and tossing it to the side.

"Why?"

"I grew up in New England. If you don't stay on top of snow removal, you'll regret it. It can bury you in backaches."

LEO

When I'd heard the scraping of the shovel out on the front walkway steps, I'd peered out of the window. What was she doing?

Was Rosanna so eager to get away from me? I might have been kind of a jerk last night, gruff one second and interrogating her the next. Did I blame her for wanting to dig out of a snowstorm to hightail it to the highway?

That's why I was better off alone this Christmas. I'd bring

everyone down. I wasn't the guy people wanted around to celebrate. I was the one to avoid as I would kill the vibe and drag down the mood.

I'd dressed and covered up with my snow gear and had gone outside to see what was going on. Shoveling. Her cheeks were pink from the cold or the physical exertion—or both. Snowflakes covered her from head to foot, lingering on her dark hair.

"You don't have to do that," I told her. "I have a plow guy."

One side of her mouth curled into a smile. "As you should in Vermont."

"I'll call him now." I motioned for her to come back in.

She continued to shovel. "I might as well finish the walkway."

I called Mitch and asked if he could come by this morning.

"Definitely not the morning," he replied with a grunt. "And possibly not today. The snow's going to keep coming down all day. We had much more than expected, and I've been plowing for much of the night. Unless there's an emergency, then I'll figure something out."

I grimaced. Could I consider getting a sexy little busybody out of my space an emergency? Nope. That was hardly a reason for him to prioritize me over more legitimate reasons, such as critical staff or those who might need access to medical care, like a woman nine-months pregnant. It definitely didn't warrant him rearranging his schedule and possibly plowing into a tree due to lack of sleep. Besides, I didn't have anywhere I needed to be.

"No urgency. Get some sleep and then come when you can."

Rosanna paused. "All set?"

I groaned. "He won't make it this morning."

Her expression was hard to read. Was she crestfallen? "Disappointed that you might be stuck here longer with a grouch like me?"

"No, of course not."

"Then what's with that look?"

"What look?" she scrunched her features.

"The one where it looks like I just told you that I don't like puppies."

She slanted her mouth into a grin. "Is that how I look when I'm thinking?"

"Guess so."

"Do you *not* like puppies?"

"Who doesn't like them?"

"People afraid of dogs." She paused. "I was just trying to figure out what this means for rearranging travel plans once more. It changes so much, I'm starting to feel whiplash." She jerked her head to the side in a dramatic rendition. Her dark hair whipped around her, some of the snowflakes flying off.

I laughed. "Funny." Then I went to grab another shovel from the shed and returned.

When she heard me shoveling nearby, she turned. "What are you doing?"

"You see, this is a shovel." I raised it in my hands. "And what you do with said shovel is shovel. It's both a noun and a verb. Whoever named it was either lazy or clever. What do you think, Rosanna?"

"Ha." She arched a brow. "Are you always so sardonic?"

"Are you always so sassy?"

Her brows knitted together. She opened her mouth but then closed it and continued shoveling.

I joined in, aware of the smile lingering on my face and squashed it. Being out here shoveling with her was more enjoyable than doing so alone. Besides, dinner was pretty good last night. Maybe I was being too hasty in forcing her to leave. Not that I had a choice in the matter; she was stuck here until the roads were plowed.

"Ready for more bad news?" I asked.

43

"What's that?" Her brows furrowed, and she adjusted her stance.

"My plow guy might make it later today, but possibly not until tomorrow."

"Oh." Her voice lowered.

"So, unless you want to cross-country ski or snowshoe to Burlington, which I don't suggest you do, it's going to be tough to catch your bus this afternoon—if they don't cancel it. I don't recommend you attempt it either. The last thing I need on my conscience is you getting caught in the elements and dying from exposure. My mother would never let me hear the end of it."

Rosanna stared at me as if trying to get a read on how I felt about that. I wasn't exactly sure myself.

She brushed a wet piece of dark hair off her cheek with her gloved hand. "Meaning I'm stuck here for a little longer?"

Stuck. That was exactly how she must feel to be confined to a cottage in the woods with a grouch like me. "Yes."

She resumed shoveling, avoiding my gaze. "Sorry about that. I know you're not pleased."

"It's fine." I grunted and resumed shoveling.

We didn't say anything else until the walkway was cleared.

"We're good for now," I said.

When we went inside the cottage, her cheeks were flushed. She pulled her hat off and her damp hair fell over her shoulders, wild and tousled. I fought the urge to reach out and touch it.

She removed her gloves and rubbed her hands together. "My hands are freezing. I can make us hot cocoa."

"Sounds good." I removed my hat, coat, gloves, and boots. I put the boots on a boot tray and dragged it closer to the fireplace to help them dry faster. Then I hung the rest of the wet clothing to dry on a clothing rack nearby. "I'll put more wood on the fire."

She removed her coat and boots and hung them beside mine.

My gaze lingered on them together. They looked kind of nice. Homey.

She headed into the kitchen and put the kettle on. After pulling out two mugs and a container of hot chocolate, she turned to me. "We should make cookies."

"Sure." Who would turn down fresh-baked cookies after shoveling? "Wait, have you even had breakfast yet?"

"No. I haven't even had coffee yet. Have you?"

"No."

She flashed a sheepish smile. "I'm revealing myself to be a terrible caretaker, aren't I?"

"Not at all." She actually had a mix of sweet and spicy I found enticing. "Now you have cookies on my mind." I glanced at the fridge. "Tell you what. How about I make coffee and scrambled eggs, and you make cookies?"

"Deal."

The cottage soon filled with the scent of coffee, eggs, and toast. The cookie dough was set aside on a cookie sheet to be baked later. We carried plates and mugs over to the dining room table.

She took a bite of the eggs. "Mmm, these are good."

"I may be a bachelor, but I can handle eggs," I said with a grin.

I stared at her from across the table. With her cheeks flushed and hair wet and wild from the snow, she looked like a siren.

She caught me staring and turned away.

Ugh. She must have thought I was a creep. I walked over to grab the TV remote. "We should keep an eye on the weather today."

Talk of the snow was all over the local news. We watched while we ate, adding comments about the snowfall and memories of other storms.

Once we were done eating, Rosanna said, "I'll pop the cookies into the oven."

While she headed into the kitchen and bent over to put the pan into the oven, my gaze followed her. I turned away before she caught me staring at her again, this time at her plush ass.

Soon, the aroma of chocolate-chip cookies had my stomach growling.

"It smells delicious in here," I said.

"Like how a cottage in the Vermont mountains should smell in the winter," she added with a nod.

True. I hadn't baked cookies here since I'd moved in over the summer. Why would I? It was just me. It was much more enjoyable sharing them with someone.

Once she took the cookies out of the oven, I headed over to grab one.

She lightly smacked my hand away. "They're too hot."

"I'll blow on it first."

"You'll enjoy them better if you don't burn your fingers or your tongue," she admonished, wagging her finger.

"Fine, I'll wait," I replied with mock exasperation and went back to tend the fire. Soon, the wood crackled with orange and yellow-ish flames, emanating heat.

A few minutes later, Rosanna came over and handed me a small plate with cookies and a steaming mug. "Coffee and hot cocoa."

"Good idea. Caffeine and chocolate together." I raised the plate. "Finally," I teased.

"You're so impatient," she countered with a grin.

"Thank you." I put the plate on the side table.

She went into the kitchen and returned carrying a plate and mug for herself. After setting them on the table, she sat on the sofa near me.

When I bit the warm cookie, chocolate oozed over my tongue. I moaned. "So good." It was heaven. Decadent.

She arched her brows. "Worth the wait?"

I caught her gaze. "Absolutely. Most things are."

Our gazes remained locked. My palms heated, and my mouth turned dry. She broke eye contact. I resumed eating my cookie, somewhat dazed. When she took a bite of hers, chocolate dripped onto her lower lip. Her tongue darted out as she licked it, and I stared at her. My heart beat faster. Damn, she was hot.

I pictured an entirely different situation with us being alone here in this cottage. One in which I wasn't the mess I was, and she wasn't here because she was being paid to put up with a stubborn grouch like me. We'd head into my bedroom where we'd warm each other up under the comforter and linger in bed. I pictured running my hands over those voluptuous curves of hers, and my cock twitched.

"Not hungry?" Rosanna stared at me.

I blinked at her, and my cheeks burned as if she'd caught me fantasizing about her. What was she asking me about? Hungry about what? "What?"

"You stopped eating the cookies. I'm guessing you either don't like them or aren't hungry."

I cleared my throat and glanced at my plate. Despite my stomach growling with anticipation earlier, I'd forgotten about them once I started to think about Rosanna—in ways I shouldn't. "Just taking my time, so I can savor the taste." Why did that have to come out sounding dirty?

I avoided eye contact while I finished the cookies, staring into the fire instead. The crackling flames seemed safer than whatever strange reaction was going on inside me.

After we finished our cookies and cocoa, we cleared up the plates.

"I better check the website for the bus company to see if they're still running," Rosanna said. "I can get the first one out as soon as the plow truck clears the road."

"Wait." I stopped her before my brain caught up. What was I doing?

"What?" She furrowed her brow.

I didn't want her to leave yet. "Maybe I was too hasty in saying no to this plan. I pushed you away before I even met you." I rolled one shoulder in a half-shrug. "Having you here isn't as bad as I expected."

Her eyes twinkled. "I'm glad to hear that it wasn't an excruciating experience."

Far from it. In fact, it was nice. Enjoyable. "Maybe we should give you being here a temporary run. Especially since we're stuck here together for an indeterminate amount of time." Would she even want to stay here after my terrible, inhospitable first impression?

She tipped her head. "What do you have in mind?"

That was a good question. I was winging this as I went. "How about three nights? That will get us to the weekend. Besides, it will be safer for you to travel as the roads should all be cleared by then."

She glanced at me for a few seconds before replying. "Sounds good."

A strange sense of relief washed over me. I glanced around the cottage. "I haven't shown you the whole place. Let me show you around."

The tour of the downstairs didn't take much time since we'd already spent much time downstairs with the seating area, dining table, and kitchen all visible in the open space. But I'd only shown her the guest room and bathroom upstairs.

"We have four rooms up here," I pointed out as we walked down the hall.

"Where's yours?" Her question sounded innocent, but when she caught my gaze again, heat grew more palpable between us. She glanced away and her cheeks turned pink. "You know, if you need me for anything."

She winced as if cringing at the possible double entendre of her words.

"I'm down there." I pointed to my room at the opposite end of where hers was. The master bedroom had been my parents, but I'd claimed it and made it my own once I moved in. It felt strange at first, but this was my home now—or at least, where I lived.

We passed a room that had the door wide open. It had storage boxes stacked against the wall. "This used to be a play-room for my sister Jeannie and me. Now it's just become a place for storage. I don't know what to do with it."

She stepped inside and turned around. "You could do so much in here. Make it your study. You could bring in a beautiful desk and matching bookshelves. Add comfortable seating. Or a space where you could work on projects." She turned to me. "What do you like to do?"

Should I tell her? I didn't see why not. "Paint."

She tipped her head, and her eyes sparkled. "Do you?"

"Yeah, you saw some of my paintings downstairs," I admitted with a shrug. I gestured to one mounted in the hallway. "Here's another one."

She stared at the painting of the snow-covered mountains. "It's beautiful. You're very talented." She turned back to me. "Those paintings of the landscapes downstairs are yours?"

"Most of them." I shrugged, slightly self-conscious. "Some in the guest room, too. I love painting the mountains and forests around here during the different seasons. But I have so many, and I don't know what else to do with them."

"You could probably bring them to a gallery," she said.

I shook my head. "I'm not that good."

"I think you are."

We continued down the hall.

"Where do you paint?" she asked.

I motioned to the closed door before my bedroom, what used to be my room growing up. "In here."

"Can I see?"

"No." My heart thumped.

She gave me a confused look.

"I don't like people to see what I'm working on."

She bit her bottom lip and nodded. "Ah, I get it. I don't like people reading my unfinished drafts. It's too unpolished."

That wasn't exactly the reason why. If she saw what I had in my studio, she'd think I was a freak.

"If you're going to stay here, Rosanna, you can't go into that room."

Her mouth dropped open. She cocked her head. "You're not serious?"

"I'm dead serious."

I should put a lock on the door. It wasn't a factor with me living here alone, but Rosanna would be here temporarily, and I didn't know if I could trust her.

She stared at me as if searching to make sure. "Okay."

"Promise me you won't go in there," I urged.

She continued to regard me as if trying to understand. It wasn't something I could easily explain. My secrets were too dark to share with anyone.

"I promise."

CHAPTER 5

ROSANNA

I returned to the guest room where I'd stayed last night, surprised that I was back. That was the first of many surprises.

The first was that Leo wasn't as grumpy as I first thought. He was actually helpful and easy to talk to—until we broached certain topics, and then he'd shut down.

The second was that he'd invited me to stay longer. Sure, it was only three nights, but considering how eager he was to get me out of the cottage as soon as I'd arrived, it was a huge step.

And the third was the room where he'd painted. Why was he so secretive about that space?

I didn't like people to read my drafts, as I'd told him, but why would his entire studio be off limits? If he was working on a painting, he could just turn the easel away from view, right? Or cover it up. It didn't make sense for him to be so private when it came to his work, especially as he was so talented.

As I sat on the plush, white comforter, contemplating this,

my phone buzzed. It was Leo's mother. "Hi, Mrs. Ricci," I answered.

"Please call me Claire," she replied. "I just called to see how everything was going. I hear my son is being his stubborn self."

I bit my lip as I stared at one of Leo's paintings of the forest hanging on the pale-yellow wall, not sure what I should reveal about this whole situation to his mother. "I think we've smoothed everything out for the time being."

"Good," she replied. "I apologize if it's uncomfortable. I didn't expect him to be so difficult about this."

I doubted that. After all, she'd arranged this without clearing it with her son, so she must have known I'd be walking into a cyclone. I kept my mouth shut about that as it wasn't my place.

"Everything's fine," I replied.

"I'm glad to hear it. If he's being mean, call me. I won't stand for that."

"Everything's fine," I repeated. I would not step in between this battle of wills willingly.

After a few more minutes of going over things, we ended the call. I settled back on the comfortable bed and exhaled. What had I gotten myself into?

I phoned Daniel and told him about the change of plans. "I'll be here for a bit after all."

"Wait, what? I thought the grump wanted you to leave. Now he wants you to stay?" he asked in an incredulous tone.

"Not the entire time. He suggested we try it for a few days."

Daniel groaned. "I don't know about this guy and his mood swings. Maybe you should book it out of there while you still can."

"Calm down, it's not like he's a serial killer. He's not that bad. He can be kind of considerate at times."

"Ooh, what's that tone?" Daniel teased. "Is there something going on there? More than you're telling me?"

"No, of course not," I denied. My cheeks heated up, and I was sure they were turning red. Yes, there were moments when I caught Leo looking at me when he thought I couldn't see him. And yes, I kind of liked how it made me feel. Fortunately, Daniel couldn't see me blushing over the phone. "You know I have a soft spot for veterans."

"Yeah, I know. Many in your family." He exhaled. "Too bad. You could have been telling me a far more exciting, juicier story right now."

I laughed. "Hate to disappoint, but there's nothing going on." A small voice at the back of my mind questioned that. What was wrong with me? I was here for a *day*. Leo didn't even want me here, so he definitely wasn't interested. He probably changed his mind and let me stay to appease his mother around the holidays, that was all.

"One day, Rosanna, you'll tell me something good. Your love life is blander than a bowl of ramen without the spice pack."

LEO

I walked down the hall from my room. When I heard Rosanna's voice on the other side of her door, I paused. Was she talking to me?

"That's not going to happen." She laughed. "I wasn't exactly expecting a warm welcome, but it's been more frigid than the temperature outside."

"Get out of there," a man said. "You can come and stay with me and my family."

"It's all right, Daniel. I'm not scared off yet. We'll see how it goes over the next few days."

Daniel? Who was he—her boyfriend? She'd denied having one, but they had to be close if he was inviting her to visit his family during the holidays.

"It's still not what they offered you. Not cool. What happened to you being there for winter break?"

"His parents set that up," she said. "He wasn't exactly thrilled about me coming and made that clear."

She didn't exactly paint me in a favorable light. Understandably so. I'd been rude since she arrived.

"I hope he treats you better. And if not, you always have a place with me."

In his bed? I winced. If they weren't a couple, they could still be friends with benefits or something like that.

Wait, why did I care? She could sleep with whomever she wanted.

"Thanks, I appreciate it, but I don't think it's necessary," Rosanna said. "I'll see you soon."

I headed away from her room before she caught me eavesdropping. What she said was right. I hadn't been welcoming at all.

Rosanna hadn't done anything to deserve this. She was only doing a job. It wasn't right to take out my frustrations on her. I needed to lighten up and try to be a little kinder.

ROSANNA

Leo was gone for much of the day. He returned to the cottage at lunch time. I offered to make him a sandwich, but he brushed it off and said he was fine.

Okay then. Was he just tolerating me in his space for three nights?

He made a sandwich and brought it upstairs. I didn't see him for the rest of the afternoon. That was fine; I could entertain myself. I read a book and did some brainstorming and writing exercises. I could at least use the next few days to my advantage, to find some inspiration here in the mountains like I'd hoped.

While I prepared chicken marsala for dinner, I listened to some upbeat music through my earbuds. I sang and danced along to "Uptown Funk" as I added mushrooms and madeira wine to the pan.

"Smells good down here."

I stopped dancing when I heard his voice over the music and spun to face Leo, who'd come from upstairs. My cheeks turned pink. He must have seen me shaking my ass. I pulled out my earbuds. "Hope you're hungry."

"Yes." He glanced at the fireplace. "I'll throw some logs on."

"It will be nice to have the fire going nearby while we eat."

Once I filled our plates, we sat across from each other at the oval table.

"How was your day?" I asked.

He shrugged. "Fine."

That was it? A one-word answer. Oh boy, this was going to be fun.

"Did you do anything special?"

He shook his head. "No, just the usual. Hiking, painting."

Ah ha, that gave me a little insight.

"What did you paint?"

"I don't discuss my work, especially while working on it."

"I can understand that," I said. "I've heard that if you talk about your art too much, you might lose your passion to create it."

He grunted and took a bite of chicken.

The conversation was strained through the meal. Maybe I'd made a mistake even agreeing to be here for three nights.

"This is really good," he praised.

A compliment. Nice. "Thank you."

After dinner, I cleaned up the dishes and put away the leftovers. He tended to the fire.

"Would you like to do anything tonight?" I asked him.

He exhaled. "Not particularly."

Okay, then. I glanced around the cottage. Although it was now dark out, it was too early for me to go to bed. I found a puzzle on the bottom of an end table. "Do you mind if I work on this?"

He arched his brows. "Why would I?"

"I don't want to bother you."

"You won't bother me."

I dumped out the puzzles pieces on the table and turned them right side up. Leo turned on classical music at low volume.

"That's a relaxing way to end the day," I said.

"I should have done so during dinner."

That would have helped with the awkward silences.

He sat on the sofa in front of the fire and read a book.

"What are you reading?" I asked.

When he glanced at me with annoyance, I thought he might throw the book at me. "An adventure novel."

I nodded and returned to my puzzle. Obviously, he was not interested in any more conversation tonight, so I continued to work on the edges.

After a few minutes, Leo walked over and watched. Then he picked up a piece and put it in.

"Want to help?" I asked.

He picked up another edge. "I can't resist a puzzle." He smiled.

Whoa, an actual smile tonight. Finally.

When he'd smile in the past, he'd quickly stop as if self-conscious about how he'd looked. He must have forgotten tonight as the puzzle enticed him.

"Besides, you picked a difficult one," he noted. "Not only do you have to complete the puzzle but solve a mystery."

True. I'd found a mystery puzzle in the closet that looked interesting. First, you put together the puzzle, having no idea what the end result would look like. Then you needed to refer to the puzzle to find clues to solve a mystery.

While we worked together, I tried to ignore how close he was—and how good he smelled. He had this outdoorsy scent about him that reminded me of the wild and remote forest setting here, one which drew me toward him. It took a lot of focus on my part not to do so and to keep my focus on matching puzzle pieces.

It took us almost until midnight, but we finally solved it.

I squealed and pumped my hands in victory. "That was close. We almost didn't make it. I've never done one of these puzzles before, but that was fun."

Leo stared at me, and I caught something in his eyes I hadn't noticed before. Desire.

Was I imagining that?

He broke our locked gaze. "There are plenty of puzzles here." Leo motioned to the closet and up the stairs.

The moment had passed, yet my skin still tingled with heat.

He cleared his throat. "I've done so many here in this cottage. After we'd finished all the traditional ones, my mother bought mystery puzzles to spice things up."

"That sounds perfect for family time." With him talking, I wanted to keep the conversation going. "Did you spend much time with your family here growing up?"

Leo nodded. "We often came up during school vacations and a month or so in the summer. In the winter, we'd go cross-country or downhill skiing, usually at Killington or Pico."

"What about the holidays?"

"A few times. But often we had to go visit other relatives. You know how it is with family obligations." He flashed a knowing smile.

I groaned. "Yes, indeed. Why do you think I'm here?"

"True. It was nice when we were here, though, just the four of us. We'd have a quiet Christmas Eve in front of the fireplace. And then on Christmas day, we'd open presents and eat a ton. We'd play games or do puzzles. No running around and dealing with traffic. No getting exhausted while preparing to feed a houseful of guests. Just some quiet time with loved ones."

"Sounds perfect," I agreed.

His gaze lingered on me for a few seconds before he turned away. I grew acutely aware of the heat simmering between us. It was so different from the piss-off vibe he exuded when I first arrived at the cabin.

When I went to bed, his blue gaze burned in my brain. He was down the opposite end of the hall. I thought of how we were alone together in this cabin. It could have been romantic under other circumstances. Despite the surly exterior, he'd opened up to me a tiny bit about himself.

Had I caused a tiny crack in his shield? And did I want to?

After all, this was simply a job. But I couldn't help remembering how he'd looked at me, and how it made me feel.

I liked it. A lot. And I wanted more.

Knock it off, I scolded myself. *You're not here for that. Do your job and focus on your novel.*

Yet, as I drifted off to sleep, it was with thoughts of Leo.

THE NEXT COUPLE OF DAYS WENT BY QUICKLY. LEO AND I WOULD eat a hearty breakfast together, and then he'd go off to do his own things. He went for a walk or cross-country skiing in the mornings and often disappeared into his studio upstairs in the afternoon. When he was up there, he often played music, not classical like he listened to in the evenings but harder rock, sometimes alternative and sometimes heavy.

The curiosity of why he was so secretive about his work still pinged at me, but I got over it. It was his private place where he liked to work. I could understand and respect that.

Besides, it left me plenty of time to work on my own projects. I sketched out ideas for characters and brainstormed plot points. Being here took off some of the pressure, perhaps because I was away from the university. The idea of writing an entire novel had paralyzed me. I'd stared blankly at an open document of a screen and then procrastinate with even undesirable tasks like laundry or mopping floors to avoid that blank page. I need to write a novel to graduate, otherwise all the time and money I'd invested into this degree might as well be for nothing.

But here, the anxiety wasn't as palpable. I sat on my bed with the curtains open, sketching out ideas in a blank journal. Or I'd go downstairs while Leo was out and sit on the sofa, gazing outside. The mountains in the distance were covered with white, appearing so majestic. The vast open space inspired me to let my imagination run free. Rather than the academic pressure in the congested city where I struggled with writer's block, here I gave myself permission to experiment and have fun.

I doodled with bright markers and sketched out character ideas. When something from a movie or a show that inspired me, I jotted notes about possible plot points and turning points. Without forcing myself to write page one of at least one hundred pages of fiction, it removed some of the stress to get out the words. After all, this journal brainstorming was still technically working on my novel, right?

I rarely saw Leo until dinner. He might have made himself a quick sandwich for lunch when I was writing in my room, sitting by a window that overlooked the snow-covered trees outside. Whenever I started to cook dinner, he'd come downstairs saying it smelled good. He'd insist on helping, or at the least, set the table or clean up afterwards.

That night, I'd made butternut squash soup with toasted croutons, and we split a panini. Leo turned on classical music and started the fire. Conversation went smoother each day, as if he felt more comfortable with me.

"Do you have any board games?" I asked.

"Sure. We have plenty in the closet." He pointed to the door near the entrance.

"Want to play one after dinner?

"Okay."

After we cleaned up, I opened the closet door and scoured the selection of old boxes at the top of the closet. "Scrabble?"

"Sounds good."

We played the game while sipping hot cocoa with Irish cream.

"Hey, you could have warned me you were a mastermind at this," I said in a good-natured tone. "My poor ego." I placed my hand on my chest.

"You're doing fine," he said.

"Please, you're killing me," I countered. "As an aspiring writer, I thought I was the wordsmith, but you destroyed me with all those little words."

"It's not so much about an impressive vocabulary as much as strategy." He pointed to his smaller words that he'd stacked up in multiple directions. Since they often included double and triple word squares, he racked up the points.

"I know, it makes sense. But I like words. I love being able to find some obscure ones using the letters on my rack."

He grinned. "And I like to win."

The victorious glint in his eyes struck me as intimate. I couldn't pull away. Heat burned in the space between us, and the tension was intoxicating. He glanced at my mouth. My lips parted, and my heart began to pound. Would he kiss me?

Did I want him to?

My body screamed yes.

He turned to the fireplace, breaking that scorching spell. I swallowed and ran my damp hands over my lap while I attempted to recover. The moment had passed.

Somehow, we finished the game, and of course, he won. I could barely form words, let alone strategize after that heated moment.

"It's getting late. I'm going to put out the fire and go to bed." I stood. "Goodnight, Leo."

"Goodnight." He didn't glance at me.

When I went to bed, I lay awake and stared out the window. The heavy, chocolate-brown curtains were pulled closed, save for a crack so I could glance outside. The moon shone high above the trees, countless stars twinkling in the night sky. Here in the mountains, away from the city lights, so many were visible. It was almost hard to believe I was looking at the same sky.

Although I tried to brush it away, I couldn't stop thinking about Leo. The way he'd looked at me had affected me much more than I wanted to admit. His gaze was downright smoldering, and it left me burning all this time later. I didn't know what to make of it. He'd pulled away, so he'd changed his mind for some reason. Whatever it was clawed at me because I kept picturing what if.

What would have happened if he hadn't pulled back? Would he have kissed me? That appeared to be where we were headed. Did I want that? Would I kiss him back?

With how my body remained overheated and tingling with desire, I'd be a liar if I claimed that I wouldn't. And now, I pictured the longing in his eyes, when his lashes lowered, and the blue of his irises darkened. In my mind, I traced the path down to his lips. A scar reached down to the corner of his mouth. It didn't strike me as hideous the way he'd claimed. In fact, it fascinated me. What he'd gone through must have been unbearable.

A part of me wanted to comfort him, if that was at all possible. He was hurting. Wounded. Alone. Isolating himself here had to be a defensive gesture. How I yearned to take away his pain for just a little while. The only problem was I didn't know how to do so.

He might not let me.

And I was almost out of time.

CHAPTER 6

ROSANNA

I didn't remember falling asleep, but when I went downstairs the next morning, Leo wasn't in the cottage. I knocked on his bedroom door to see if he was in there and wanted breakfast. No answer. Then I knocked on the room beside his. No answer there either. I lingered there, hesitating. The urge to open the door to see what he was hiding on the other side grew strong. What could he possibly have in there that he had to keep it a secret?

Various scenarios tumbled through my mind. He could have some sort of torture chamber. He could be a serial killer just toying with me before he dragged me in there by my hair. I released a nervous laugh. I didn't believe that. Not with what I knew about Leo so far. All it would take was a turn of the knob, and a quick peek. I placed my hand on the doorknob.

A scraping sound startled me, and I jumped away from the door as if it were on fire.

My heart pounded as I hurried down the stairs to see where

it had originated. Leo was outside, shoveling the walkway. If he had walked in and found me invading the room I'd promised not to enter, how would he react? My hands turned clammy. Curiosity had almost gotten the best of me.

I opened the front door a crack. "Good morning."

He stopped shoveling and stood, staring at me for several long seconds as if assessing me. For what? My pulse escalated once more, and I wasn't sure why. Was it because of that almost-kiss last night? Or because I could have been caught poking where I shouldn't be?

Likely both.

"Good morning," he said.

"Should I come and help shovel?"

"No. It's not much more than a dusting. I'll be done in a few minutes."

"Have you had breakfast?"

"No."

"I'll make you something." Before he could protest, I closed the door.

I searched through what we had for food to see what I could prepare. Hot oatmeal with peanut butter, bananas, and cinnamon. Yes, that would be perfect to warm up after shoveling snow.

By the time Leo came inside the house and removed his coat and boots, it was almost ready, just simmering on the stove.

"Damn, woman," he said with a grin that made my skin heat. "Every time I walk in here it smells so good. I'm going to miss you—" He sneered and cleared his throat. "I'm going to miss your cooking when you're gone."

My cooking? What was he about to tell me?

Ha, why would I dare think that? His feelings toward me might have evolved from repulsion to tolerance, but that didn't mean I could come up with any schoolgirl fantasies that wouldn't go anywhere. After all, I was leaving tomorrow.

"I can leave you some recipes," I said.

After he washed up, we sat at the table and ate breakfast.

"It's my last night here," I said.

His mouth twitched, but he didn't say anything.

"Any special requests for dinner?"

He leaned back in his chair. "You've cooked for the past three nights. It's my turn."

I pushed my hair out of my eyes. "That's one of the things I was asked to do—prepare meals."

"That was the deal you made with my mother, not me." He motioned to the living room. "Relax. You've done enough cooking for me. Don't worry about doing anything else today. I'll let you know when dinner is ready later."

I blinked at him. "Are you sure?"

"I wouldn't have said it if I wasn't."

"I'll clean up the dishes."

Why was he being so nice to me today? Was it because of last night? Maybe he felt uncomfortable, but he hadn't done anything. He hadn't tried to kiss me.

I glanced at his lips and suppressed a sigh. No doubt about it now—I wished he had.

After breakfast, I went for a walk in the woods. The scent of pine and and clean mountain air invigorated me; it even tasted pure with a crisp sensation on my tongue.

The sun dappled through the boughs of the trees, casting gray shadows on the snow. I trudged through paths where the snow wasn't as thick, which was easy to find as Leo's footprints led the way. The forest was quiet, yet full of life. Birds chirped and wind rustled the trees. An occasional sound of darting through brush or breaking twigs indicated small creatures lived nearby.

I pictured some of Leo's paintings of this scenery, the way he'd been able to capture the textures through his brushstrokes. It reminded me of watching a Bob Ross episode. Whenever I thought Bob Ross was about to make a drastic mistake as he cut through a painting with a vivid splash of paint, he'd surprise me and end up creating something that blended seamlessly into the painting. Is that what Leo did when he painted? Did he do so fearlessly, visualizing the outcome in his head? I'd love to watch him paint but couldn't see that ever happening with how secretive he was about his artwork.

I followed his boot prints through the snow until I grew weary and then turned back toward the cottage before I overdid it. The gray stone of the cottage blended into the sky. Although I'd thought the stone exterior cold and imposing when I'd first arrived, I now pictured the cozy space within. The warmth of the fireplace. The glow of embers. The soft lighting for reading and relaxing classical music. And the scent of whatever I'd cooked that day. It was kind of fun to be able to create meals there, whereas back home, I'd more likely create something quick while dashing to or from campus or pick something up while I was out.

When I entered, I announced, "Hello?"

Leo didn't answer. He could be upstairs painting in the studio, but when he was up there, he played music, so I guessed he was out. That was common as he often disappeared for most of the day.

I didn't see him until late afternoon. I was reading a mystery on the sofa when he walked in with a bag of groceries.

When I stood to help, he stopped me. "Stay put. I'm cooking tonight, remember?"

I'm sure the look I gave him appeared perplexed. "Okay."

I filled a glass with water and returned to the living room. Soon, the fragrant aroma of tomato sauce and cheese reached me.

"Wow, that smells good," I said. "What is it?"

"Don't worry, it's edible," he teased, not answering me.

"Is there anything I can do to help?" I cleared my throat.

"No. I'll let you know when it's ready."

Less than an hour later, we sat across from each other at the dining room table, and he served me a huge plate of chicken and eggplant parmesan. We ate dinner and talked. I told him about my walk, and he highlighted his favorite things about the changing seasons here. I sensed him less standoffish and more willing to talk to me.

"This is delicious," I said. "Maybe we should've had you cook the entire time."

"See, I can take care of myself. I'm even able to cook something that's somewhat nutritious." He flashed a boyish smile.

"Leo, you have a nice smile." I hadn't mentioned it until now.

He scowled. "You don't have to say that."

"I'm saying it because it's true."

He pointed to his scar. "I've seen what it looks like. It makes me look like a freak."

"No, it makes you look happy. Genuinely happy. And I like seeing you that way." I reached over and touched his hand.

His mouth remained downward, but he didn't argue. He glanced at my hand on his. Heat curled inside me. I shouldn't have left my hand there. I'd meant it as friendly gesture but couldn't help feeling there was more intimacy to it. Was it because of this odd attraction growing between us?

I pulled my hand away. No point in delaying it. My time here was almost up, so I better make plans and not overstay. "There's a bus leaving tomorrow afternoon at one. I should get to Boston before dark."

Leo's face dropped.

"What's wrong?"

"What are you going to do when you get back there?"

I rolled a shoulder. "I'll probably crash with a friend for a night or two and then look into other options."

It was too bad this gig hadn't worked out, but Leo promised to pay me for an extra two weeks for my inconvenience.

"Will you end up visiting your father?" he asked.

"No." I shook my head with adamance. "Since I already got out of that situation with my stepfamily, I'm not going to volunteer to go. I'd rather stay home alone and read. Treat Christmas like any other day."

LEO

It was amazing how quickly the three days flew by with Rosanna there. I'd let my mother know that I was giving it three days as a compromise. She urged me to continue it through the holidays, but I wouldn't relent. Yet, when Rosanna mentioned the bus tomorrow, my chest tightened.

I thought we were having an enjoyable time here, but perhaps she was just acting. Maybe she was eager to get out of here, and the three nights that she already stayed here were unbearable.

"Something wrong?" Her brows pulled together.

"Well, I was just thinking of these few days as a trial run. And you know, it wasn't bad." I shuffled from one foot to the other. "It's been okay having another person around. And since you don't want to go to your family for the holidays, I was thinking…" My voice trailed off. "Do you want to stay the full time like you'd planned?"

"Really?" Her lips parted and eyes widened with a surprised look.

"Yeah, but if you've had enough, I get it. I can be a bit much."

"No, that's not it. I was thinking you couldn't wait to get me out of here, so you can get back to having your privacy."

I grunted. That's what I thought, too, but the past few days with Rosanna changed my mind. "Since we'd both be alone on Christmas otherwise, I thought it might be kind of nice to spend it here with another person." I didn't say with her specifically, and I'm not sure why. We'd spent so much time together, and the underlying sensual tension had been potent—unless I'd fabricated it all in my head. Maybe I was afraid of coming on too strong.

That was possible since she was paid to be here as a caretaker. This was a job for her. I meant nothing to her.

Avoiding eye contact, I took a swig of wine and put down the glass. "I know I was a jerk when you arrived. I wouldn't blame you for wanting to leave, but I'm hoping you can forget about my stubbornness and stick to my mother's arrangement."

"What made you change your mind?" she asked.

I fumbled with the stem of the wine glass. "I don't mind having you around." With a shrug, I added, "Besides, it's the holidays, and I should do something to make my mom happy, right?"

Was I babbling? My hands felt hot and clammy. Finally, I raised my gaze to meet hers. "Do you want to stay?"

CHAPTER 7

LEO

 My heart pounded as I awaited Rosanna's reply. She searched my gaze as if trying to read my intentions.

"I'd love to stay." She put her phone down on the table.

"You would?"

"Yes." She smiled.

My skin tingled with warmth. I didn't know what to do with my hands. "Okay. I'm going to head upstairs."

I said goodnight and walked up to my room. It was better to get some distance from her before I said or did something to change her mind.

THE NEXT DAY, I WENT CROSS-COUNTRY SKIING. WHEN I returned to the cottage, Rosanna had her laptop on the sofa in the living room with some books on the side table. She liked working there during the day as the sunlight spilled in through the open windows, which provided a splendid view of the mountains and forests.

"How was skiing?" she asked.

"Good." I kicked the snow off my boots onto the boot tray and removed my hat and gloves. "I'm sweaty and need to take a shower."

She nodded, her gaze lingering on me.

That gaze sent heat down to my groin.

"Enjoy." She turned away, slightly pink, as if questioning why she'd said that.

I took the stairs, thinking about her and that look. While the water warmed, I stripped. I removed my boxers, semi-erect. Once I stepped beneath the hot water, I leaned forward, letting it cascade down my back. I pictured the way Rosanna had looked at me downstairs. It wasn't the first time she'd glanced at me that way. Could she possibly feel desire for me, the way I did for her?

While I washed, I wrestled with my feelings. Although I'd tried to deny it from the first day Rosanna had stepped into the cottage, it wasn't something I could lie to myself about much longer. Not when every part of me seemed to light up when I saw her. I was getting used to her presence here. No, not just that. I liked having her here.

But it could also be torment. How could it not when we'd spend each evening together? The delicious dinners, the soft music, the fire in the fireplace, it was downright romantic. I should cut that crap to not scare her off, but she didn't seem to mind.

She took such good care of me. Yes, she was being paid to do so, but I sensed she did so as well from the goodness in her heart.

When we played a game in the evening, sitting close, her scent teased me. I wanted to lean in and inhale the vanilla and cinnamon scent that reminded me of Christmas morning. And then taste her. Would her lips be as delicious as every other aspect about her?

Whenever I went to bed, I thought about her down the hall. What did she wear to sleep? Did she ever think about me?

I sure as hell thought about her often, fantasizing about what we could do if she was here for a different reason. If she was here because she wanted me, too.

If she was with me in my bed…

Fuck, I was raging hard now. There was no denying it—I wanted her.

I closed my eyes and pictured the way she looked at me. How her pupils would widen, and her lips would part.

Damn, I couldn't go back down there like this. I fisted my erection and stroked it as I thought of her. I wanted to touch her, taste her, make her moan. I yearned to hear my name on her lips as I made her shatter.

It didn't take long until I was rubbing myself harder and faster. As a climax rushed through me, I dropped my head forward and groaned. Fuck, that was louder than I anticipated. Hot white streams shot into the swirling water.

I hoped she didn't hear me over the running water. What would she do if she heard me jerking off? Would she take off?

Or would she join me?

Yeah, right.

I glanced down at the left side of my body. She hadn't seen these scars, only my face. The rest of me wasn't pretty either. One side of me at least. I was still in shape, though. Skiing, hiking, and chopping wood helped there. But that didn't take away the scars, the vicious marks that left my skin lined and puckered with dark, angry welts. Even though they'd faded, they remained a permanent symbol of an incident I couldn't remember but had changed by life and others in a flash.

Why would someone as beautiful and kind as her want someone as ugly and damaged as me?

She wouldn't. No one would.

AFTER I GOT DRESSED, I RETURNED DOWNSTAIRS. WHEN I HEARD her talking to someone, I stopped.

"How's it in the cottage?" A man's voice asked.

It sounded like the same guy she'd talked to before.

"Not so bad. It's very nice here. Cozy."

"And how is the grouch?"

My muscles tightened. She must have described me that way. Judging by the way I'd acted toward her in the beginning, I couldn't say she was wrong. Still, I wasn't crazy about her telling someone about my prickly personality.

"Not too bad either." She laughed. "We're getting along fine."

Who was she sharing info about me to?

"That's good. I was ready to come and get you."

"No need," she said. "It's all good."

"How's your project coming along? Are you finding the quiet break there helping you as you hoped?"

She sighed. "Still in the brainstorming phase, I'm afraid. I have some ideas brewing. What about you? How's the visit with your family?"

"I'm enjoying break and not working over the holidays. There's plenty of that ahead next semester. You should have come with me to my family's. We're doing a lot of eating and drinking."

My interest rose. Whoever this guy was that she was speaking to was close enough to invite her to spend the holidays with his family—and they'd love to meet her. My gut tightened.

"Maybe another time," she said.

"When you get back, let's meet up. We can go over our ideas. Give each other tips.

I scowled. Yeah, I bet he would like to give her a tip of something in particular.

What was wrong with me? I wanted to get a better look at her screen. Shame slithered. Why was I spying on her?

No, not spying. Just being curious. She was a woman sitting in my home. I had the right to know if she was hiding something, right? It would simply be a basic safety precaution.

Ding dong, went the bells chiming me out on my bullshit excuse.

I took a few light steps down, so she wouldn't hear me approach. It was difficult to see what was on her laptop screen from this angle, but I glimpsed the guy she was talking to. He appeared to be early to mid-twenties with slicked dark blond hair and a handsome face. No imperfections, no scars. Young and carefree.

A dagger of jealousy stabbed me. Was the pretty boy her boyfriend? Or just a friend she hooked up with?

Either way, I hated it. I slipped back up the stairs before being caught spying.

I was a fool to think she'd ever be interested in me and was misinterpreting her kindness as something more. I wouldn't do that any longer. I'd simply enjoy her company but not dare think that it could lead to anything else.

AT BREAKFAST THE NEXT MORNING, I ASKED, "HOW ARE WE DOING with our food supply?" I knew the answer already.

She laughed. "I think you're pretty well stocked, but we can go and pick some things up to keep us going." Her eyes brightened with a conspiratorial glint. "Maybe even pick up something a little more festive for Christmas."

"Like a feast?"

She arched a brow. "For just the two of us?"

I shook my head. "Yeah, that's a bit much."

She clasped her hands, and her eyes widened. "We can do it. There are no rules that state you need a minimum number of people for Christmas dinner."

"True," I agreed.

"So, let's eat, drink, and be merry," she suggested.

"Okay." Although I hadn't planned on celebrating at all this year, a small dinner with Rosanna wasn't too much.

It didn't hit me with the same reservations as would a giant family gala. After all, the guys I'd served with wouldn't be home celebrating the holidays with their families ever again. Survivor's guilt made it difficult for me to be able to embrace what was stolen from them.

As I grew more comfortable with the idea, her enthusiasm grew as well. I shared some memories of happier times I'd spent in the cottage with my family over Christmas break.

I glanced up toward the ceiling. "We probably still have decorations in the attic."

Her face brightened. "That would be fun to decorate."

I pointed to the picture window with the trees stretching in every direction. "Take your pick."

Rosanna bit her lower lip. "We're going to chop one down?"

"Yes."

"Oh, I've never done that before."

"Don't tell me you're one of those people who puts up an artificial tree?"

She gave me a look. "Not when I was young. We used to go and pick a tree with my mom at a scouts' stand. But after my dad remarried, my stepmom hated the messiness of all the needles falling. With her, it had to be artificial and tidy." She groaned. "None of the handmade ornaments from when I was a kid deserved a spot on the tree. Like I said, she had her own particulars about appearances, and homemade ornaments do not have a place in that regard."

"I see." I stood. "Get ready to go outside. We're going to get a tree."

"Really?"

"Really."

"I'll grab an ax from the shed."

Her brows furrowed. "Wait, I feel bad. I'd be picking out a tree for slaughter."

I laughed. "We'll pick one that needs to come down anyway," I assured her. "And if it makes you feel better, I'll plant another one this spring. Or three."

She smiled, and it brightened her face. "Okay."

AFTER WE PICKED OUT A PINE TREE, WE CARRIED IT BACK TO THE house. My mother had loads of Christmas boxes still stored there, so I found a tree stand and we set it up.

"We'll let it settle tonight and then decorate it tomorrow. I found ornaments upstairs."

Rosanna smiled. "Perfect." She tipped her head. "I was thinking of making grilled cheese and tomato soup and biscuits tonight. What do you think?"

"Sounds delicious."

"Maybe we can watch a Christmas movie after dinner, something light and fun."

"Sure. *Home Alone? Elf?*"

Her eyes brightened. "Ooh, I love them both." She bit her lower lip. "*Elf.*"

After dinner, we sat on the sofa and ate popcorn as we watched the movie. Having Rosanna beside me as we laughed at the familiar scenes took away some of my trepidation about the holidays. After all, it would simply be another dinner with just the two of us, right? No different from any other evening since Rosanna arrived.

It wouldn't change anything.

CHAPTER 8

ROSANNA

"*L*eo, be careful," I said as he backed down the ladder after adding the star to the top of the tree. My gaze lowered to his ass.

He laughed. "Don't worry, I'm barely off the ground. Even if I slip, it won't be a far fall."

Leo stepped off the ladder and away from the tree without incident. "How does it look?" He gestured at the pine tree we'd set up and decorated, the star almost reaching the ceiling.

"Perfect. I think we pulled off a Christmas Eve miracle." I inhaled. "It's even smells and sounds like Christmas in here."

That was courtesy of the fragrant tree, the simmering scent of apples and cinnamon from a blend I'd heated up on the stovetop, and the holiday playlist coming from the wireless speaker.

It had been a quick scramble to get the cottage decorated in time for Christmas. We'd pulled down boxes marked "Christmas" in the attic and decorated the tree with garland, lights, and ornaments. What I loved about them were that many were handmade and hardly two were the same. Some included pictures of Leo as a child. He was so cute, especially in the ones with him missing his front teeth yet staring at the camera with a goofy smile. This was what I missed about decorating the tree, the small homey touches that signaled family.

After a slow start with Leo appearing to humor me, he started to get into it. The trinkets stashed away in boxes brought back memories, which he shared with me. It warmed my heart. He revealed more each day, appearing to trust me.

"The miracle hasn't been pulled off yet." Leo motioned to the kitchen. "We still need to prepare for the feast."

"We'll manage," I assured him with a confident nod. We'd gone food shopping earlier. It was the first time the two of us had gone anywhere together. At first, we tiptoed around each other, somewhat awkward with us being strangely polite. On my part, it was because of how intimate this activity seemed, like we were a couple. Also, I sensed his unease at being out in public with his scar on display. The speculation in people's eyes as they tried not to stare made him apprehensive. His mouth would tighten, and his body emanated more tension.

After the initial discomfort in the supermarket faded, we then bickered lightheartedly. Which cereal was best, which bagels to buy, which food was essential for Christmas. We agreed to bake a turkey, sweet potatoes, mashed potatoes, a green bean casserole, salad, and dinner rolls.

We stocked up the cart with food for the feast and staples with each of our favorites.

Leo stared at the tree and then turned to face me. "I couldn't have pulled this off without you." He grunted. "I wouldn't have even tried." His blue eyes sparkled with an appreciative glint.

He looked content. I loved seeing him like this.

"It was nothing," I brushed off with a wave. "Besides, it was fun."

"Thanks for staying here and putting up with me, Rosanna."

"You're more than welcome." When I met his gaze, I froze.

He stared at me with more warmth than I'd ever seen. And something else I didn't dare try to define.

The air between us heated. The space was palpable. All those looks and the closeness from the past few days coiled up into a heady moment. Something seemed to have shifted. A barrier broken down.

Leo's gaze lowered to my mouth. I couldn't move except to part my lips. I was drunk on my desire although I hadn't touched a drop of alcohol.

My heart pounded from my chest cavity all the way up through my ears, swallowing out all else.

Leo leaned down. My pulse shot higher than the star on the tree, higher than the tip of the stone chimney.

He blinked. Then he broke eye contact and turned away.

What? That spell broke, and I remained dazed.

He cleared his throat. "Is there anything I can do to help with the pie?"

"Pie?" What was he talking about? I finally figured it out "Oh. Of course, the blueberry pie."

I'd made such a fuss about how we had to have a blueberry pie and insisted that we get the right kind of blueberries—the tiny ones from Maine. That was how my mother had made her blueberry pies for every holiday.

"No, I think I can manage," I added. "I need to make the dough first and let it chill. My mother didn't add sugar. She said the way she made it was sweet enough." Why was I babbling?

"Okay." He searched around the cottage. "I'll—um—start the fire."

Judging by the heat simmering inside me, he already had.

He strode over to the fireplace. My gaze locked on him until I came to my senses.

Pull yourself together.

Yes, that's what I had to do. I opened the fridge and then paused there, staring at nothing in particular but grateful of the reprieve with the cool air. What had just happened?

I blew out a slow breath. Okay, we had another moment. One we shouldn't have had. It was probably instigated by the intimate setting and the holiday ambiance and the intensity of being alone with someone I was attracted to. Did he feel the same way about me?

We had other moments with that searing eye contact over the last few days, but never any as intense as what we just had in which I thought we might kiss.

Still, I had to be rational. Practical. After all, his parents had hired me to make sure he was okay. He was hurt. Maybe even shattered. He'd come here to have the time and space to heal.

What he didn't need was a complication with someone like me developing a crush on him.

If I was truthful with myself, I didn't need that complication either because I'd be returning to school in a few weeks. If I let myself grow attached to Leo, then I'd only make it more difficult when I eventually had to leave.

LEO

What was wrong with me?

I lit the kindling for the fire and stared at it as if it would burn some sense into me. I should not have made a move on Rosanna. Yes, I'd stopped myself before anything happened, but I doubt there was any way not to notice I was about to kiss her. The briefest flicker of fear in her eyes snapped me out of it.

Although, I thought she felt something, too, thought there was desire in her gaze, it woke me the hell up. No way in hell did she want that. She didn't need me coming on to her like some creepy, lonely man.

Now what? Should I act like it never happened? Or would that attract more attention to the elephant in the room?

We managed to avoid each other for the next hour or so. I headed upstairs to my studio while she prepared the pie in the kitchen. I couldn't hide there for long because it would make the situation more uncomfortable. It was Christmas Eve, and we'd spent all day hustling to make it a festive celebration. I was supposed to be preparing Christmas Eve pasta, which had been a tradition in my family.

We'd had a great day decorating and preparing for a quiet Christmas celebration. As we'd gone through the boxes of decorations from the attic, I'd shared tidbits about each. Since we were out in the woods, I'd made ornaments out of pine cones—far too many. She insisted we hang them all up, noting they were perfect for the ambiance.

I had to man up. If I hid in my study all night, it would make what happened a bigger deal and harder to recover from. It would make things worse.

I headed out of my studio to prepare dinner downstairs, and her bedroom door was closed. Ah, damn it. Was she trying to get her distance?

Or worse, packing?

Ah shit, did I spook her out, and she was leaving?

I ran my hands through my hair. If she stuck around through Christmas, I'd have to keep my distance and act like a perfect gentleman.

I played the Nutcracker suite as I prepped dinner. Since it just involved cooking shrimp and pasta, it was an easy enough dish.

At the sound of her bedroom door opening upstairs, I froze. What next?

She came down the stairs wearing an emerald green

sweater that looked soft to the touch. It hugged her full breasts just enough to tease—not that I should be looking—and her black pants were snug on her lush hips. My mouth was parched. Did she have any idea of the effect she had on me?

I dared to meet her gaze.

She smiled. "It's snowing again!"

Relief flooded me. She didn't look ready to bolt. She looked happy, and that radiated all the way over to me, filling me with warmth.

"Is it?" I'd been so preoccupied with myself and preparing dinner that I hadn't paid attention. I glanced out the large picture window. It was difficult to see in the dark, but it was indeed snowing.

"I love a White Christmas." She inhaled. "It smells great down here."

She seemed happy. Maybe I didn't blow it—yet.

"It's just about ready. Hope you're hungry. I made enough for a family."

She tapped her stomach and laughed. "We didn't have lunch earlier, so I'm guessing we can make a serious dent."

"You don't think the cookies counted?" I arched a brow. We'd eaten plenty as we'd decorated.

She shook her head and laughed. "Nope."

I filled our plates with hearty helpings and carried them over to the table, which was now covered with a red tablecloth and plaid place settings. "Wine?" I asked her.

"Yes, please."

We'd stocked up on wine and spirits while out shopping. Now I wondered if that was a mistake. I'd have to keep my guard up so as not to do anything stupid—like tell her how hot she looked tonight.

During dinner, she carried most of the conversation, bubbling over how happy she was that we'd chosen to celebrate

Christmas. I was too. It was a million times better to have her here than to be alone.

After we cleared up, she asked, "Do you have room for dessert?"

"I think I had too many cookies already and have a sugar overload." With a smile, I added, "But I can't wait to taste your pie."

Holy hell. I closed my eyes and grimaced. That came out sounding far too dirty. I reopened my eyes and clarified. "Your blueberry pie." Groan. Somehow that made it sound even worse.

A slight smile curled up at her corners of her lips. "How about a game?" she suggested.

"Sure." I shrugged. "Your choice." A game would give us something to do and talk about besides thinking about her and how close she was.

When she headed over to the closet and leaned onto her tiptoes to reach a game, her sweater rose. My gaze locked onto the few inches of smooth skin exposed at her lower back. What would it be like to touch her soft skin? Kiss her?

Stop it. Thinking like that will make the situation worse. And all the more difficult.

She returned to me with a teasing smile. "Monopoly. I am *so* going to destroy you at this game, Leo."

"Oh, you think so?" I arched my brows. "Challenge accepted."

One thing I loved about her was her competitive streak and playing games. Although she was so sweet and caring, the second a board game came out, so did the knives. She took no prisoners. When we played Sorry the other night, she wasn't one bit apologetic about taking me out.

We set up the game. I claimed the race car and she the thimble.

"Who picks thimble?" I teased.

"Me," she declared. "I'm banker."

"How do I know you won't cheat?"

"How do I know you won't?"

"Because I'm a SEAL. We're trained with honor. Discipline."

"Does that mean you don't think I have either of those things?" She posed.

"Oh, we'll see, Miss English major."

"It's creative writing major," she clarified.

"It's all words, isn't it?" I leaned forward and teased, "Not that it helped you in Scrabble."

"Oh!" Her mouth turned into a wide *O*. "Is that how you're going to play, Leo Ricci?" She lightly punched my arm.

I grabbed her arm and laughed. "Now you're playing rough?" I teased.

"I have another arm." She raised her other arm and barely tapped my chest.

"Do you now?" I took her other arm.

As she attempted to squirm out of my hold, we ended up tumbling together on the sofa. This was more than we'd ever touched each other before. I ended up on top of her, leaning over as she gazed up at me, panting. An excited gleam in her eyes captivated me. Her pupils dilated, lips parted—so close, so tempting.

Remember what happened earlier.

It took all my restraint to pull back.

"Leo?"

"Yes?" My voice sounded strange, unlike my own.

"Don't pull away." She leaned up and brushed my lips with hers.

Every cell in my body jolted to life. Our touch started tentative and then exploded with fiery need. I cradled her head in my hands as I lowered myself onto her.

Need pulsed through my blood, roared through my veins. A

warning flashed in my brain, like a giant billboard—I could scare her away.

She released the most delicious sounding sigh. I wanted to hear more. I want to be the one to make her moan in pleasure.

I wanted more.

CHAPTER 9

ROSANNA

I was kissing Leo. My body danced with jubilation. His lips were gentle at first. After he cradled the back of my neck in his hand and pressed his hard body against me, his mouth was more insistent. So good.

He tasted like spice and wine. He smelled like the forests and mountains. He trailed his fingers down my neck and down my side, and my skin tingled with heated awareness. I wanted to savor every moment of this: the sound of the crackling fire, *The Nutcracker* playing in the background, and the comfortable warmth from the fireplace. I couldn't believe I'd been the one to initiate this. It wasn't like me.

Wait, *what* was I doing? I shouldn't be kissing him *at all*.

I pulled away and gasped for breath. "I'm sorry," I stammered and slid out from beneath Leo to as far as I could get at the end of the couch. My body screamed in protest, but I had to be rational. "I got swept up in the moment but shouldn't have done that." Staring at the Monopoly game we'd set up but hadn't even started, I tried to find some sense to get myself in check. "Raincheck on the game."

"Sure." Leo stood and avoided eye contact.

"It's getting late." Leo slapped his thighs and stood. "I'm going to bed. Good night."

"Good night."

He didn't even look at me before he headed for the stairs and took them two at a time, no doubt wanting to get away from me.

I lowered my head into my hands. "What a mess." Why did I do that? I totally flirted and then kissed him. How messed up. I thought he was going to kiss me, and my body heated with anticipation. When he pulled back, I couldn't let it go. It would drive me crazy.

So I kissed him. Ugh.

His parents hadn't hired me to seduce him. Leo didn't need this, and neither did I. Coming here was an opportunity to escape my family. I didn't need to add a new complication to our already tenuous arrangement.

I headed up to my room and closed the door, acutely aware that he was down the other end of the hall. Only two doors separated us. Great. This would be a strange night and an awkward Christmas morning.

Sure, he'd kissed me back—and it was amazing—but should I be surprised? He was a man. I'd been hit on in college enough to know that men were happy with just one thing, and that wasn't what I wanted. I didn't want a fling. I didn't want a relationship either. I just wanted to be able to get through the holidays and then move on with my final semester.

Since I initiated, it was on me to put it behind us if we wanted to enjoy Christmas.

I THOUGHT I WAS THE FIRST ONE UP THE NEXT MORNING WHEN I woke up early. But when I went downstairs, the coffee was already made. Leo left a note saying he went for a walk.

I grunted. He was probably trying to get away from me. I didn't blame him.

He said to have breakfast without me. I'd make my mother's apple cinnamon pancakes anyway and make enough for the both of us. It would smell like apples and cinnamon in here, the way Christmas morning should be.

While I baked them, I called Daniel to wish him a Merry Christmas. After he told me some of the highlights of his relatives being annoying or outrageous on Christmas Eve, he asked about mine.

"Um, it was quiet," I said. "And interesting."

"Interesting, eh?" His tone edged higher in speculation. "I hope that means what I think it means."

Tapping my fingers on the counter, I debated what to tell. "I kissed Leo," I admitted.

"I knew it!" he declared.

I groaned. "This isn't trivia night, and you don't get any points for it." We'd played every Thursday at a bar near campus.

"No." He laughed. "But it is *knowing-what-Rosanna's-not-telling-me*. I could tell you were interested by your tone whenever you talked about him."

"You could?" I bit my lip. "Was I that obvious?"

"To me, because I know you all too well. What happens now?"

I dropped my head back. "Awkwardness, most likely. I need to apologize when I see him this morning."

"For kissing him? Don't be ridiculous. I'm sure he wanted it as much as you."

I groaned again. "Doubt it. Remember who we're dealing with here. He lives like a hermit and didn't want anyone here. He's probably just tolerating my presence."

91

When I heard the front door of the cottage open, I said, "Got to go," and ended the call.

Leo walked in and fixed a gaze on me. I tried to read his expression, but it wasn't easy. His face was a mask of neutrality. Was he trying to keep his distance?

I forced a cheerful, "Merry Christmas."

"Merry Christmas." His lips twitched into a semi-smile.

"I made apple cinnamon pancakes. It's a tradition in my family."

"Thanks," he mumbled. "Maybe later. I'm not hungry."

Not hungry? He hadn't turned down anything I'd made since I'd arrived. We must have really screwed things up last night.

"Leo, I'm sorry about last night. I don't know what happened. I guess I just got swept up in the vibe." I motioned around the cottage. "You know, the wine, the fireplace, the warm cozy cottage with the snow falling outside. And of course, Christmas Eve."

He grumbled. "Don't worry about it. I was just as much to blame. Forget it ever happened."

Forget it? That was like asking me to forget what fire looked like. Impossible. How could I forget how wonderful that kiss had been? I might be able to move on from it, but I don't know if I'd be able to *forget* it.

"Okay." I clucked my tongue.

"You're right. The ambiance doesn't help." He searched around. "We should go get some fresh air."

I cocked my head. "Isn't that what you just did?"

"Yes. But it's the romantic vibes like you said." He huffed. "Do you want to do something outside?"

Leo was right. We'd spent too much time alone together in the cottage and could use the break outdoors. I'd gone for walks since I'd been here but not with him. "Like what?"

"With all the fresh snow last night, it's a good morning to go cross-country skiing."

That would be a first on Christmas morning. Interesting. Still, it was better than tiptoeing around each other inside the enclosed space of the cottage.

"I don't know how. I've only gone downhill skiing," I replied.

"It's not hard. I can show you."

Leo brought a couple pairs of boots up from the basement. "These are my mother's and sister's. See if one fits."

I tried them both. His sister's pair was a better match. Once we got bundled up in our jackets, hats, and gloves, we carried the skis and poles outside.

It was magical outside. A white Christmas. A light breeze sent snow cascading from the trees. I stuck my tongue out and captured some.

Leo stared at me. Then he turned away and swallowed. "You're going to want to move like this." He popped his boots into his skis and pushed himself forward. "It's more of a glide than a walk." He displayed it with exaggerated movements and then skied back to me. "The tricky part is attaching your boots to the skis." He pressed his pole to the area before his boot and popped it out. "Bend your foot and press the tip in like this." He showed me and his boot connected again with a clicking sound.

I tried but no luck, so I tried a few more times. My foot pressed against the lever thing, but nothing happened. "Am I doing something wrong, or is mine broken?"

"It looks fine. Watch me." He repeated the process, showing me how to bend the tip of my foot while also pressing to lock the boot in.

"You make it look too easy."

"It is once you get the hang of it. But—" he paused, "you need to get the hang of it first." He flashed a sly grin.

That smile was progress. Maybe we were putting the awkwardness behind us. Leo's suggestion to do something physical outdoors was smart. It was a better idea than fantasizing about something physical we could do indoors.

I stared down at my boot, my new nemesis. "Easier said than done."

After several more frustrating minutes, I managed to get my right foot in. "Halfway there," I declared and pumped a gloved fist. Eventually, I got the other one connected as well.

"Perfect." He pushed himself ahead in the snow. "Now push your weight forward just like this."

I attempted to do so. It wasn't smooth like him, but at least I moved forward. "Am I doing it?"

"You're getting there. Remember glide."

"Glide," I repeated, and then shuffled ahead with jerky movements.

"Have you skated before?" Leo asked.

"Yes. Several times."

"Think of the movement more like ice-skating rather than downhill skiing."

"Okay." I exhaled and tried again. As I pushed forward on each leg, I held my weight longer on each side for more of a glide. Although it wasn't great, it was progress from the shuffling I was doing moments ago.

"Yes, that's it," Leo praised. "You're doing great."

I wouldn't say great, but it was movement. Besides, it was less frustrating than connecting to the skis. Eventually, I was more comfortable with the motion. I followed Leo's tracks as he pushed a path through the trees.

When we paused, I was panting. My heart beat hard. "Wow, this is more of a workout than I expected."

He chuckled. "It is more grueling than you'd think. An excellent workout."

"If a former SEAL is saying that, then I'm pretty impressed with myself."

"You should be." He fixed a warm gaze on me. "You impress the hell out of me, Rosanna."

My cheeks warmed at his praise.

He took a deep breath and inhaled the mountain air. After reaching into his pack, he handed me a water bottle. "Make sure you drink some of this, so you don't get dehydrated."

"I thought I was the one supposed to be taking care of you. Now you're taking care of me?" I grinned.

"Yes." His eyes twinkled. "If you'll let me."

There was something heavy in his tone, something that affected me deep within. I took a long swig of water and then declared, "Cross-country skiing. This is something new for Christmas."

Leo grinned. "That's the way it should be, right? You keep your favorite traditions and then make new ones."

I arched my brows. "Is this a tradition with you?"

"At this rate, I'll take things as it comes." He shrugged. "Who knows? It could be."

After another sip, I closed my water bottle.

"Ready to go head back?" he asked. "We can warm up in front of the fire."

"I don't think I need to warm up. I am ridiculously hot."

"I'll say," he muttered and then appraised me.

"What?"

"Nothing." He smiled. "I was just agreeing with you."

I bit my lower lip. Leave it to me to say something to bring back the sensual undertone—what we both appeared to be trying to avoid all morning.

Time to divert. "I can't wait until we start our Christmas feast."

LEO

Rosanna and I skied back to the cottage. When we spotted the stone house, she sighed. "Home sweet home."

I glanced at her, happy she thought of it that way—at least while she stayed here with me.

Both of us were hot from exerting ourselves, yet the air cooled our faces. Her cheeks were as red as I'm sure mine were, which unfortunately tended to highlight my scar.

"This part's easier." I showed her how to pop off the skis using the pole and it went much quicker than learning how to connect them. Then we carried our skis and poles to the front door.

I shouldn't have made that innuendo about her hot. She hadn't said it that way, but then I went there. How could I not think that way after seeing the fire in her eyes last night, when I had her voluptuous body pressed to mine? I needed to scrub that hot kiss from my brain if I wanted to be able to function around her and not think of taking her in my arms again, but that was impossible. Besides, that was a memory I wanted to keep with me always, even if it brought me the pain of loss one day.

After all, she'd be leaving to return to school in a few weeks. She'd be gone from my life forever.

"Smells like Christmas in here," Rosanna declared with a wide grin.

"It does indeed."

The scent of the tree and spices filled the room.

"I'm going to put some things in the oven to heat," Rosanna said. "While that's happening, I'll go up and take a quick shower."

"Okay. I'll have it covered down here."

I already showered first thing in the morning. A cool shower was a good way to get my blood moving and wake me up for the day. With the way we'd worked up a sweat while skiing, I could do a quick rinse off as well. After all, I wanted to smell good for her.

Why? The small voice inside asked. *Nothing is going to happen between the two of you. It was just a fluke last night. Probably just curiosity. That's why she stopped. It's not going to happen again.*

"Can you put on one of those Christmas records?" Rosanna asked. "We need to have the ambience, right?"

"Absolutely," I agreed. While she worked in the kitchen, I pulled out one of my family's old Christmas albums, a Frank Sinatra one.

Soon Frank's melodious croon filled the room. Rosanna hummed to "Have Yourself a Merry Little Christmas," and then sang along.

Her voice filled my head, her happiness affecting me. She brought a light to this dark cottage. Whereas I wanted to just hide away like a Grinch avoiding all the townspeople, Rosanna brought Christmas to me.

She removed oven mitts and put them on the counter. "Okay, you think you can hold down the fort while I go take a shower?"

Why did she have to put that image of her in the shower into my head again? I grunted and then nodded my head with vigor.

As she climbed up the stairs, I stared after her. When she was out of sight, I slapped my cheek. *Get a hold of yourself, man.*

I went into the kitchen and pulled out some appetizers that we could nibble on, starting with a shrimp cocktail. The sound of the water upstairs started. I glanced upward. Upstairs, she'd continued to sing the same song.

How was I supposed to ignore her when I heard her singing with that melodious voice? When I knew that she was naked and standing beneath the hot stream of water? As she raised her arms to wash her hair, her breasts would lift. So tantalizing. I rubbed my jaw but couldn't stop picturing hot water running over her full breasts. It would trail down her belly and farther still. Behind her, the water would roll down her back and caressed the round curves of her ass.

Don't think about it. Don't think about her, I chastised myself.

How would I get through the day here alone with her when I couldn't stop thinking about her lips? How they'd felt pressed against mine last night. So soft and satin smooth. The delicious scent of her enveloping me. The light touch of her fingers.

How her curves pressed against mine.

Great, now I was semi-hard in the kitchen while preparing for Christmas dinner. I need to snap out of this. I walked over to the kitchen sink and turned on the faucet. I splashed some cold water on my face.

"Ouch!" she shouted from upstairs.

I bolted up the stairs to the bathroom door. "Rosanna, are you okay?"

"Yes. The water got super-hot for a second, and it surprised me," she said from the other side of the door.

"Shit, that was me. I turned on the cold water. Sorry." The plumbing here was old. I might have scalded her.

"It's okay."

"Do you need anything?" I asked. Dear God, why did my voice sound so low and gravelly? What would she possibly need my help for in the shower?

"No, I'm fine. I'll be out soon."

"Okay." I pressed my hand on the wooden door. What was I doing? Stalling? Waiting? Perhaps hoping for something more?

I was out of my mind. It wasn't like she was going to invite me in there with her. I stepped away, my fingers lingering on the door until I forced my feet to move away from her.

The more distance I put between us, the better. Safer. It was already hard enough to spend all this time with her under the roof. As much as I loved having her here, maybe this whole thing was a mistake.

As soon as I got downstairs, my mother video called. Talk about a reminder to get my act together.

"Merry Christmas, Leo! How are you?"

"Great, great. Merry Christmas, Mom." I glanced down at her ugly Christmas sweater. That wasn't her usual style of nice slacks and blouses. "Nice sweater."

She chuckled. "Your sister got it for me. And one for dad, too. She said we all needed to wear them today."

I grinned. "That sounds like one of her ideas."

My mother's dark brows lowered. "Is everything going okay with Rosanna there? I know you weren't happy about it, but I'm hoping you've come around."

"Everything's fine," I interrupted, not meaning to cut her off. "Say Merry Christmas to everyone for me."

"You can do so yourself. Hold on. Everyone, say Merry Christmas to Leo."

I resisted groaning. She turned the camera to show my family. The second I saw everyone and heard their well wishes, my mouth curled up into a smile.

Seeing everybody was wonderful. A part of me felt a pang of loss for not being there with them. No, I was better off here. Besides, I was actually looking forward to the celebration Rosanna and I'd planned. So far, we'd pulled it off, aside for the little snafu with our kiss last night.

My mother turned the camera back on her. As I paced through the cottage, she asked, "Is that a Christmas tree?"

"Yes, Rosanna convinced me to decorate. We put the stuff out from the attic."

"Oh." My mother's eyes twinkled as if she realized something.

My cheeks felt warm. "It was easier than trying to argue her out of it," I added in a gruff tone.

After we talked some more, I wished everybody a Merry Christmas once more and ended the call. At the sound of feet descending on the stairs, I turned. Rosanna wore a red velvety top over black pants. Her curls were slightly damp, and she wore light makeup that accentuated her eyes and lips. She looked radiant.

"You look festive," I pointed out.

"Good." She beamed. "It is Christmas, after all."

It was indeed. And I hoped I'd get through the day without doing something stupid that would ruin it.

ROSANNA

"Let the feast begin!" Leo declared after he finished slicing the turkey.

I laughed. "With just the two of us here, we're going to have leftovers for days."

"Good. Turkey sandwich leftovers are the best."

He placed the tray of turkey with the other dishes on the counter. The mingling aromas of all the food, including mashed potatoes, sweet potatoes, a green bean casserole, and veggie dishes stirred my appetite.

"One more," I added and put out a plate of cheese *bereg*, inhaling the heady aroma of baked cheese. "My grandmother on my mother's side is Armenian. I'm a mix of Portuguese, Armenian, English, and more. This recipe is my favorite dish she'd made. It has cheese and parsley in phyllo dough. She folds them into triangles, but I did the quicker version in layers. Still, delicious."

"Where does she live?"

"California with my grandfather."

"Do you ever visit?"

"Yes. It used to be every year, but now, not as often." I was overdue for a visit. I'd be sure to call them later today and wish them Merry Christmas. I'd called my father earlier. He still didn't understand why I wasn't there but didn't focus on that too much, for which I was grateful.

What I was even more grateful for was that the awkwardness from last night's kiss with Leo didn't cast a shadow over our celebration today. Yes, we'd tiptoed around each other that morning, but once we started preparing the meal, we became more comfortable again. There was a lingering glance that brought the blood rushing to my cheeks, but Leo turned away and said he'd set the table.

I clapped my hands. "Oh, we almost forgot the wine." I retrieved the chilled bottle from the fridge and poured us each a glass.

We filled our plates and sat at the table the way we'd done most nights, but now we had the festive decorations and the tree.

While we ate, we gushed over how delicious everything was.

"Tell me about your favorite Christmas," he said.

When I thought back, a wistful expression had to have come over my face. "It would have to be any of them with my mother. She loved Christmas so much." I glanced down.

"Oh, I'm sorry, Rosanna," he said. "I didn't mean to make you sad."

"No, you didn't," I said, blinking back tears. "I want to think about her. This was her favorite day of the year." I motioned to him. "What about yours?"

He glanced around the cottage. "I'm remembering one in particular that we had here. I must have been around nine or ten. Santa got me a pair of skis, and I couldn't wait to try them out. I went skiing with my family the next day, and it was awesome."

"And look at you now, still skiing."

He shrugged. "You need to make the most of the snow. It's better than staying cooped up inside."

"But it's warmer inside." I smiled and then took a sip of wine.

We ate until we were stuffed and then went for a walk outside to have a break before dessert. The newly fallen snow clung to the tree branches. With the sunlight dappling through the trees, it leant a magical glow to our surroundings. I moved closer; it was like my body gravitated toward him. I was keenly aware of how close his hand was to mine. If I leaned closer, our fingers would brush.

I inhaled the fragrant pine-scented air. "It's so beautiful. No wonder you loved celebrating Christmas here."

"I like the peacefulness of the forest," Leo replied.

It was quiet compared to the city but not silent. Birds sang and insects chirred. An occasional sound of scurrying in the distant indicated small animals nearby.

I picked up a pine cone that had fallen into the snow and shook it off. "Oh, I have an idea. Pine cone ornaments, like the ones you made when you were younger."

He chuckled. "Aren't we a little old for that?"

I shook my head. "You're never too old for that." I reached over and touched his arm. "It would be nice to give them to each other and hang them from the tree. Homemade gifts are the best."

"Sure, why not?" He glanced around and then walked over to pick up a fallen pine cone. "I found mine."

When he glanced at me with a victorious glint in his eyes, my insides tingled once more. How would I make it through the next few weeks without succumbing to this attraction?

Weeks? After remembering the heat in our kiss last night, how would I make it through the day?

After a couple of miles or so, we returned to the cottage. I went up to my room to make some more calls. When I returned downstairs, Leo had put on "A Christmas Story" on the TV.

"Ooh, I love this movie!" I gushed.

"We can have it on in the background as we make the ornaments." He brought his brows together. "You're serious about that?"

"Sure." I shrugged. "It would be fun."

Besides, having something to do with my eyes and hands would keep me focused.

"I'll be right back then." He dashed upstairs and returned a few minutes later with glue, glitter, and yarn. "I found these in storage. The glue might be dried up, though."

Fortunately, it wasn't, and we were able to decorate the ornaments. I covered the edges of my pine cone with red glitter.

"For you." I handed mine to him with a smile. "Merry Christmas, Leo."

"And for you." He handed his to me.

"Thank you." I glanced down at the pine cone he gave me with silver glitter. "Let's hang them up."

We headed over to the tree and searched for a spot. While I reached to put my ornament up high, he'd leaned in to hang his. My breast brushed against his chest. Jeez, that slight contact was too much; my nipples tightened to hard peaks.

"Sorry." I avoided eye contact while I reached up to the branch. Still too short, I moved up to my tiptoes.

"Let me." Leo put his hand on mine.

Another flash of electricity rushed through me. I let go of the pine cone. He hung it up where I'd been trying to reach, then he bent down and grabbed his and moved it up closer to mine.

"There. That looks better." He grinned and then glanced at me.

Our gazes locked. The smile left his face as a more intense expression took over. I couldn't move, couldn't talk. So much tension simmered between us, I was ready to implode.

His blue eyes darkened with a hungry gleam. My lips parted, and his gaze lowered to them. My heart pounded in my ears with a steady thump-thump, which I was sure echoed throughout the cottage.

Leo dipped his head. I leaned up on my tiptoes as if firing on instinct rather than sense. Our lips brushed. Softly. Gently. But then the fire raged.

We kissed with a blistering intensity. He pulled my body against his, and I wrapped my arm around the back of his neck. We devoured each other with a fierce hunger, as if finally unleashing that desire we'd struggled to reign in for so long.

He ran his hand down my side, down to my ample hip, and

then back up, sliding over to cup my breast. I sighed against his mouth. It felt so good to have him touch me the way I'd craved.

Our tongues tangled. He tasted of wine and the spices of our meal.

"Oh Leo," I murmured, pulling away a fraction as I gasped for breath.

When I kissed him again, I trailed my fingers over his jawline. I cupped his cheek without thinking, my fingers running over the rough lines of his scars. He froze.

I pulled my fingers away and pulled back. "Is it okay to touch you like this?"

A fearful glint appeared in his eyes. "You don't want to do that." He stared at me, never looking more vulnerable.

"I want to touch all of you." Gently, I cupped my hand over his unmarred cheek and then the scarred one, searching his frightened eyes.

He didn't pull away, but his breath came in rasps. He appeared to be wrestling with something. Insecurities? Demons?

After removing my hands, I leaned forward. I kissed his forehead and then his cheek without the scars. Then I kissed the scarred one. He remained frozen.

Maybe we needed to slow things down. I pulled away slowly, but then he surprised me by pulling me back into a heated kiss.

He ran his hands down my hips and around my butt, squeezing it. "I've wanted to touch you since the first day you were here."

I jerked my head back. "You have? I thought you hated me being here."

"I wanted to but couldn't. Probably to protect myself."

We stared at each other again, our breaths still ragged. Revealing our insecurities appeared to bring a new under-standing between us. My mind raced with the intensity of what just happened. I wanted him so much but didn't want to push too soon after he'd coped with me touching his scars.

While my heart pounded, my skin tingled with heat. I searched around the cottage and tried to focus on something normal. The blueberry pie sat on the counter, waiting for us.

I turned back to Leo and cocked my head. "Do you want a breather? Maybe some dessert?"

He lifted my hand and kissed the back of it while glancing at me. "Hell no. I don't want to wait for you any longer, Rosanna." The dark hunger returned to his smoldering gaze. "I'd rather have you over any dessert."

Heat blazed inside me as if he'd thrown lighter fluid onto the burning logs. I nodded, not sure I could even speak. "Yes," I managed in a breathy voice. "Yes."

CHAPTER 10

LEO

*a*s I led Rosanna into my bedroom upstairs, my heart thundered. I'd wanted her for so long and had struggled to suppress that yearning. But now I had her in my arms, kissing and touching her, like a fantasy come true.

The light was off in my room but the illumination from the hallway light let me see her. When I reached beneath her soft red sweater and touched the satin over her breast, my cock throbbed against my zipper. Her nipples were hard beneath the silky fabric. As I started to pull up her sweater, she sucked in a breath.

I pulled away from her sweet lips. "What's wrong?"

Her brown eyes, so full of desire moments before, flashed with a vulnerability. "I'm a little self-conscious about my body."

My eyes widened in surprise. She was curvy and gorgeous. Unmarred. Unscarred. "But you're beautiful."

She pursed her lips with a doubtful expression. "I'm not exactly the tall and thin model type."

I couldn't believe this. "Is that what you think I want?"

She lifted a shoulder and rolled it. "I don't know. Is it?"

"No." I shook my head. "I've wanted to touch all these luscious curves and kiss these beautiful lips." I touched the bottom one. "Every inch of you tempts me, Rosanna. I want *you*."

A small smile spread across her face. She pulled her sweater up over her head, and her brown, wavy hair tumbled over her shoulders. As I took in the image of her here in my room, my mouth went dry. Her full breasts teased me as they pressed against those satin cups of her bra in a vivid red that was a shade darker than her sweater. I ran my finger over the top of her mounds.

"So soft." I bent down and kissed above her breasts. The fragrance of vanilla and cinnamon grew more pronounced. She always smelled so good. This tease of her flesh stoked my raging inner fire. I ached for more.

Reaching around her back, I unfastened her bra. She slid the straps down her arms and tossed it to the hardwood floor.

The sight of her with her breasts exposed almost paralyzed me. "You're gorgeous. I want to touch you."

Her eyes were hooded now, dark with desire once more. "Do it," she urged.

As if I'd ignore that delicious invitation. I leaned her onto my bed, and her dark hair spilled over the pillow. I kissed her mouth, her jawline, and her neck as I caressed her breasts. Kissing and licking down her body, I captured one succulent bud in my mouth and moaned. My cock throbbed with a renewed vigor.

"You've got me so hard," I murmured against her soft flesh.

"Let me feel it," she said. She reached down and stroked my shaft.

A low, guttural moan escaped me. "You're going to kill me."

She reached up and pulled my shirt out from my pants. "I want you, Leo."

My body turned rigid. This was the moment that ruined everything in my fantasies—when I'd reveal my monstrous side. I'd found ways to cope in those visions by keeping the light out or my shirt on. Now, the light was out in my room but the one from the hallway provided illumination and wouldn't hide me.

She hadn't recoiled when she touched the bad side of my face. She'd even kissed it. I didn't think she did so out of morbid curiosity. It affected me deep within, and I still didn't know how to process it.

"I have more scars," I revealed. "All along this side." I motioned to my left flank. "They're vicious. Ugly."

Rosanna tilted her head. "We're all afraid of being exposed. But you don't need to hide from me," she said in a gentle tone. "Is it okay if I unbutton your shirt?"

Fear galloped from my gut to my throat. I didn't want to hide from her and ruin this. After all, she'd expressed her self-consciousness and then revealed herself to me.

"Yes." My voice came out strangled.

She kept her gaze fixed on my face as she unbuttoned my shirt. With each one undone, she trailed her fingers over the exposed skin on my chest. And then farther down.

When the shirt was completely undone, I held on to the bottom of it, my last chance of shielding myself. Rosanna bent down and kissed my chest.

A protective shield I'd been hiding inside for so long cracked. She kissed down my torso and then moved back up to my face. When she kissed my lips, she opened my shirt a few more inches and pressed her bare breasts against my chest.

As we kissed, more defenses crumbled. For whatever reasons, she wanted me, and so far, I hadn't scared her away.

She slowly slid my shirt off one shoulder and then paused, as if waiting to see if I was okay. I was surprised that I was. Slowly,

I removed the shirt from my unmarred side first but then held my breath as I exposed the scars.

Rosanna continued to kiss me. She ran her hands down my back and then back up. Moving her fingers with gentle sweeps over my body both ignited a fierce heat and allowed me to gain more confidence that this would be okay.

She rounded her hands over my shoulders and slowly down my arms while I touched every part of her I could reach. Then she touched my chest. With gentle movements, she raised a brush fire along my skin as she descended down my core. Her fingers spread, edging toward my sides.

I pulled my mouth a hair's width away from hers, waiting for her reaction as her fingers reached the rough edges. Would she yank her hand away in horror?

Her fingers fluttered over my scars. She didn't recoil and snatch her hands away.

"It's okay," she murmured, her breath tickling my lips.

I believed her. Somehow with her "seeing" with her fingers before her eyes made it easier. Her fingers trailed over the vicious raised marks.

"I'm sorry this happened to you," she said. "But I'm glad you're here with me."

So much emotion rushed to the surface, a strangled sound escaped me. God, how I wanted her. I captured her mouth with mine again, devouring her and leaning her back onto the bed. I kissed down her torso as her eyes took on a hooded gaze and then I pulled her pants over her hips. She arched her body and wiggled the pants down. I edged them over her legs and pulled them off her feet before tossing them to the floor.

With just a pair of tiny red panties, she stared at me with hunger, despite how my scars were now clear to her. Her gaze traveled down to them, but she didn't flinch.

The worst was over.

I released a choked breath. While she watched me with her beautiful eyes, I unfastened my pants and pulled them down.

I moved back over her body, touching her soft tanned skin. When I kissed along the top of her satin panties, she squirmed. I moved between her legs, licking her thighs. The scent of her desire increased my throbbing need. She moaned and curled her fingers along the hair at the back of my neck.

"Oh, Leo." Her voice was barely a whisper.

"Tell me what you want." I kissed her mound.

She sighed. "You. I want you."

Slowly, I slid her panties down. Then I couldn't wait any longer. Her fragrance teased me, and I had to taste her. With a slow lick up her wet slit, I moaned in relief, which was mirrored in her drawn-out sigh.

Fuck, she tasted so good. I swirled my tongue inside her and slipped a digit into her wet flesh.

"Yes." She squirmed beneath my mouth, moving her body as if desperate for more.

That's what I needed, too. Craved. I licked and fucked her with fingers as she writhed against me. As she moved faster, my intense hunger for her grew. I'd never wanted a woman like this before. I wanted to bring her pleasure over and over again.

Her breathing grew more ragged, and her body tensed.

"Oh my God, I'm right there," she cried.

She arched her body and released a breathy sigh. Her walls clamped over my fingers, and I slid them out. Sweet honey coated my tongue. She was the most delicious thing I'd ever tasted.

When she came down from the high, I pulled away.

"Fuck, you taste so good," I said in a low rumble.

She reached for me, eyes hooded and dazed. "I need you," she cried.

"One second." I pulled my tented boxers down, and my cock sprang free.

She gazed down at it, eyes widening with appreciation.

I reached over to my nightstand and fumbled inside for a condom. I didn't think I'd need one after hiding out here but was glad that I'd shoved the ones that I'd had in there.

As I sheathed myself in one, her hooded gaze raked over me. I never thought a woman would look at me with such desire again.

Once I was covered, I slid back into her arms and rubbed my shaft in between her wet folds.

"Please," she begged, reaching down to grasp my shaft.

As she edged it toward her opening, I positioned it there.

When I breached the entrance, my head dropped forward. "Fuck." I pushed in a few inches. She was so tight, but the wetness eased my way.

I gave her time to adjust as I penetrated inside. When I was fully entrenched, she wrapped her arms around my waist.

Gliding out, I then rocked back inside her. She moaned in pleasure. I thrust in and out of her, harder each time. She matched my movements from below, arching her beautiful body up to meet mine.

It felt so good, and it had been too long; I was already about to explode. No way. Not without making her come again. I wanted to feel her tighten around me.

I slowed my movements. "What positions do you like?"

"This is good." She clenched my lower back.

I lifted her hips and rocked in and out slowly. "Do you like to be on top?"

She bit her lower lip and glanced at me as if uncertain.

"I want to make you feel good, Rosanna. Tell me what you want."

"Let's switch," she agreed.

We adjusted positions. She covered her stomach as if shielding it when she straddled me.

I reached up and caressed her cheek. "You're beautiful." I

trailed my fingers down her neck. "Nothing will turn me on more than watching you. I want to feel you come all over me."

She nodded and then ground down on my cock as if bolstered with that confidence. We both moaned as she took me deeper inside her.

She glided up and down. I held onto her hips as I bucked into her from below. Her movements grew more intense, faster.

As she ground, I sensed her body tightening again. She was getting close.

"Come for me, baby," I encouraged.

"Yes." She moaned.

She rode harder and then tipped her head back. Her face contorted and then relaxed with rapture as she fell forward. Her tightness pulsed around me, and I didn't stand a chance of holding back.

A climax roared through me, rising in intensity like a tsunami. I released a fierce cry as I grasped her hips and exploded deep inside of her.

CHAPTER 11

ROSANNA

hat a night. I woke in Leo's room, his arm draped around me from behind, and blinked my eyes open as I adjusted to the light. I'd never been inside Leo's room before and had only seen glimpses of the dark furniture and navy-blue and green plaid quilt when the door was ajar. The walls were painted a tree green with more of what I gathered to be his paintings of the Vermont wilderness. The furniture was dark and masculine without any clutter on top.

He breathed slow and heavy behind me. I snuggled back against him, cocooned by the warmth of his body. I traveled back to last night, replaying each delicious moment here in bed. He was so skillful, taking me to a level I'd never been. My lackluster experiences in college didn't lead me to believe I could ever soar and feel such pleasure.

What affected me even deeper was the emotional connection. We'd revealed such insecurities about ourselves, leaving us both exposed and vulnerable. He'd bared his scars to me, something he was so self-conscious about. He let me touch them. The violence that his body had endured, still lingering with those physical reminders, almost brought tears to my eyes. I'd struggled to hold them back, so as not to bring him additional pain. He'd already gone through so much.

Last night had been so magical, so emotional, but what did that mean for Leo and me now?

And more importantly, what did each of us want it to mean?

I was only here for a few more weeks. Would we spend that time as lovers and then each go our own way? Come mid-January, I was leaving the cottage and returning to college. I didn't see any way of this relationship continuing, if it was even that.

Come on, now, you should know better. You slept together. It doesn't mean anything more than that. Haven't you learned that by now?

But it seemed like what we had last night was more than just sex. It had to be with that emotional connection.

Or maybe I was just setting myself up to get hurt. I took a deep breath and exhaled. It was better not to let myself put too much into it. Try to think of this like a fling rather than anything more.

When the urge to go to the bathroom lured me to climb out of bed, I moved as gently as possible to slip out from under Leo's arm. Fortunately, my bare feet met a plush area rug rather than cold hardwood floor. I gathered my discarded clothes and then walked naked down the hall, unable to avoid the coolness of hard wood this time, and then I tossed my clothes onto the bed in my room.

While in the bathroom, I hopped into the shower. As the hot water streamed over my hair and down my body, I remembered how good it had felt to have Leo run his hands and mouth down me. I traced my fingers over my skin, picturing the way he'd done. How I wanted him to touch me like that again.

I lathered and then rinsed off with cooler water.

Back in my room, I pushed the door, but it didn't close. While I toweled off and got dressed, music came up from downstairs. It was Leo Armstrong singing "'Zat You, Santa Claus." Leo was awake and must be in a good mood. I smiled, eager to greet him this morning.

As I brushed my wet hair, the next song played, and I froze. It was Elvis Presley's "I'll Be Home for Christmas."

My breath came in faster. No, I could hold it off.

Could I? My body trembled as I sank to the bed in slow motion. The memories seeped through my veins, winding up like vines crawling and tangling my brain.

I'd been so good yesterday; it was the first Christmas where I didn't spend some time alone with a good cry. I suspected part of that had to do with the newness of being here and celebrating with Leo. As the first tear fell, I readied for it. Spending Christmas with him had been a remarkable distraction, a happy occasion, but it didn't prevent the memories from tumbling into me with the force of a tidal wave.

A sob racked through my body. It had started, and now nothing would hold back the tears.

LEO

When Rosanna turned off the water in the bathroom upstairs, I finished cooking the omelets. Then I poured a cup of coffee to bring to her.

A shaky sob stopped me on the stairs. Was she—*crying?*

I listened. She was indeed. Her pain hit me like a grenade in the gut.

Continuing up the stairs, I glanced through the crack. Rosanna had curled up on her side. Her body rose and fell with each sob. What had caused her sadness?

I swallowed. Did it have something to do with me? I thought

last night had been incredible, and that she'd think so, too, but maybe I was wrong. Perhaps she'd slept with me out of pity and regretted it today.

My jaw hardened. I should have expected that. Why would a gorgeous woman like Rosanna, who had her whole life ahead of her, want anything to do with a broken beast like me?

"Rosanna," I said in a low tone to indicate my presence. "Are you okay?"

She sat up and rubbed her red, glassy eyes. "I'm sorry, I didn't want you to see me like this."

I stepped inside and offered her the coffee.

She brushed her tears away and accepted the cup. "Thanks." She took a sip and put the mug down on a coaster on the nightstand.

I bent my head. "Was it what happened between us? If I came on too strong last night, I apologize."

"No." She rubbed her eyes. "It's not like that. Last night was amazing." She pulled her knees up to her chest and wrapped her arms around them. "It's Christmas in general. I have a hard time with it." She sniffled. "Or I have ever since..." She took another shaky breath. "I thought I'd gotten past it this year, but it caught up with me."

"Why?" I stood nearby, not wanting to encroach her space.

Rosanna lowered her knees and took another sip of the coffee. She took a deep breath, and when she exhaled, her body appeared to shrink. "Because—" She paused. "Because it reminds me of my mother." Her bottom lip trembled, but then she inhaled and tipped her chin up. "She loved Christmas. More than anyone I've ever known." Her eyes gleamed with more tears.

I reached over to the night stand and offered her a tissue.

She dabbed her eyes. "She'd spend all of December decorating the house, and then on Christmas morning, she'd be the first one up. She was thrilled to watch me open gifts. And then my mother, father, and I would have a huge breakfast—apple pancakes, sausage, and fruit salad. We'd be stuffed until dinner and then eat some more." She cracked a smile.

I wished I could do something for her. "It sounds like it was wonderful."

"Yes." She bent her head. "She loved listening to Elvis's Christmas albums." She sobbed again. "When I heard 'I'll Be Home for Christmas,' it hit me hard. My mother loved to play it. She'd told me she listened to it while she was deployed when I was a toddler. She missed her family and consoled herself with a promise that she'd be back by the next one. She played it every year, wistful. But she won't be home for Christmas anymore, and that guts me." Her voice croaked. "I miss her so much." Tears rolled down her cheeks.

Raw emotions hardened my muscles. My jaw tightened. I'd been the one to play the song, trying to continue the festive vibe through this morning, but instead, I'd ruined it and sent Rosanna into tears.

Was there anything I could do to fix it?

"I'm sorry. I know that's hard." I swallowed.

She nodded, staring at the quilt.

"I know what it's like to be away from home during the holidays. It's tough." Guilt swarmed within. I had the opportunity to be with my family but had denied it. I thought I was doing what was best for others, but maybe I was being selfish. Did I have any fuckin' clue what was best for anyone? With the way Rosanna cried before me, clearly not.

"I'm sure you understand what she went through better than I do." Her tone was gentle.

"Perhaps." My voice came out strangled. I didn't know what to say, what to reveal, and most important, how to help her.

"Like you, I'd been looking to just get through the holidays. I usually search for distractions as it's not the same without my mother. But the time we'd spent celebrating was wonderful.

Although I thought of her often, I was okay with it. We were having such a splendid time, and I thought I put it behind me. But I must have been delaying the inevitable because once I heard that song, all these emotions that I kept buried welled up." She motioned to her chest and then spread her fingers. "It hit me like a tidal wave." She lowered her hand. "Every year, I think it's a little easier, but maybe I'm wrong. Because I crumbled." She flashed a wan smile. "I guess I don't have it together as much as I'd like."

"What you're feeling is human." I sat beside her and cupped her cheek "And I know exactly what you mean."

"You do?" She cocked her head and searched my eyes.

My throat tightened. "I know what it's like to lose someone. To miss someone." My voice came out low and measured.

I felt so much for her—and for so many others. The guys who I served with who wouldn't be home with their families, not this year. Not any year. They weren't coming home again ever.

Survivor's guilt had clawed at me since I'd realized I was alive while others weren't. Why me and not them?

Seeing the effect on Rosanna, it slammed into me how their families would be suffering. Not just this year but forever more.

"Oh, Leo, I'm so sorry." Her voice sounded pained.

My gaze drifted off as I remembered. I brought it back to her. "Why?"

"Because I can see how whatever I said has affected you." She wiped her eyes abruptly with the back of her hands. "Just forget I said anything."

"No, I don't want to do that. You got me thinking is all."

"Do you want to tell me?"

Did I? She'd revealed such heartache. I couldn't shield my pain like an unfeeling robot and shut her out. I took three deep and measured breaths. "When I was injured in a blast, we lost two men. This is the first Christmas their families will be without them." I lowered my head. "I understand the guilt and the grief. Part of me thinks I shouldn't be celebrating with my family while they can't. I didn't want to visit my family and darken everyone's mood."

She bit her lower lip and gave me a sheepish look. "And I coerced you into celebrating."

I stroked her cheek. "I'm glad you did. I'm conflicted, no doubt. Another part of me knows I can mourn but also live." My fingers trailed down her soft cheek and then I lifted her chin. "Just like you do. Just like your mother would want you to."

She nodded. Her eyes watered, and tears rolled down her cheeks. I wiped them away.

"Come here." I opened my arms and invited her to lean into my chest.

She cradled against me, and I wrapped my hands around her. I kissed the top of her head. Her vanilla-scented shampoo filled my nose, and I inhaled it more deeply.

What I just told her about living her life made me a hypocrite because I was here hiding out. As I held her, and she sobbed against my chest, I vowed to take care of her if she'd let me. She'd helped me more than she'd ever know, and I didn't know how to tell her.

I rubbed her hair and murmured, "It's going to be okay," and hoped it was true.

ROSANNA

I hated crying like this in front of Leo, but as he held me against the soft flannel of his shirt, he comforted me. He smelled so good, that woodsy scent that reminded me of the Vermont forest and mountains—of him.

He rubbed my back, soothing me. "It's all right, Rosanna."

I lay against him for a long time until the worst of the pain subsided. Although I'd thought he was a rude jerk the first time

I'd met him, nothing resembled that now. He was so kind and gentle and considerate.

What he'd told me about the guilt he'd felt about celebrating hit me hard. He'd endured so much. Reason took over, and I realized I shouldn't be crying against his chest.

I pulled away from him. "I'm sorry." I gave him a nervous smile. After rolling my shoulders back, I attempted to get a hold of myself and blew out a rough breath. "I'm supposed to be here for you. I shouldn't be saddling you with my issues, and making you feel like you need to comfort me."

Leo stared down at me with warmth in his eyes. "It doesn't have to be one sided."

"What do you mean?"

He pushed my hair from my damp cheek. "We can be here for each other."

The gentleness in his gaze was so sincere, it affected me deep in my core. Hope alighted inside me. "Yes," I agreed.

We searched each other's eyes. The dark memories we'd revealed had left us both feeling exposed. I was drawn to him more than ever. It wasn't the fierce desire like the sensuality that had built up between us last night, but a desperate need to connect with him. He recognized my pain, experienced it, felt his own. Like he said, we could be here for each other.

I reached up, my hands trembling, and dared to touch his face again, both the unmarred side and then the one with the scars.

He tensed. A frightened glint captured his eyes.

I whispered, "Together." Then I heaved out another sigh and leaned toward him. My eyelids lowered as we moved together, and my heart rammed hard against my ribs. Every inch of me tingled with heated anticipation.

When our lips brushed, it was simply magical.

CHAPTER 12

LEO

*a*fter the initial worry about Rosanna regretting sleeping with me, she'd shared the real reason. Her pain drove me to want to care for her more, the way I'd promised, just as she'd done for me. The quiet Christmas with her hadn't just helped me get through the holidays but had made it wonderful.

Unforgettable.

I didn't think I'd ever be able to enjoy Christmas again. She showed me how I could, albeit in a different way. Christmas brought her heartache as well. She hadn't wanted to celebrate either. Our quiet, subdued Christmas together turned out to be exactly what I didn't know I needed.

The next couple of days passed in blissful perfection, and we couldn't keep our hands off each other. Although the days had stretched on one after the other before Rosanna had arrived at the cottage, now they whizzed by so quickly. Too fast. I wanted to slow it down to avoid the goodbye that was inevitable.

When Rosanna made breakfast the next morning, she wore soft pink pajama bottoms with a fountain pen and ink on them and a black sleep shirt. I nuzzled the back of her neck. "The only thing I want to eat right now is right here."

She giggled and then tipped her head aside, granting me more access. "Let me turn off the stove so the oatmeal doesn't burn."

I waited for her to do so. Once she turned toward me, I lifted her up and propped her onto the counter.

"Oh," she uttered in surprise.

I moved in between her legs and kissed her neck. As I moved my mouth down her body, she released a low whimper. I loved drawing those delicious sounds out of her.

When I pulled down her pajama bottoms, she edged her ass up, and I slid them off her body. The scent of her arousal pushed my semi-erection the rest of the way. With her exposed to me, I buried my head in between her sweet thighs and tasted her delicious essence.

She ran her fingers through my hair, emitting soft moans as I pleasured her. Soon, she was panting and grasping onto the edge of the counter.

"Leo," she murmured, drawing out my name on a low sigh. "I'm right there."

I knew she was. In such a short time, I was already learning what turned her on, what she liked, and how I could bring her the pleasure she craved. I loved everything about this. Her taste, her moans, the look of rapture on her face. I loved how she submitted to me and let me explore all the ways I could satisfy her.

I loved—

No, I wouldn't say it. Wouldn't think it. Why make it harder when she left? What we had was now. There was no future.

I increased the pressure with my tongue. Her body coiled

tighter and tighter still. Then she unraveled with a desperate cry.

As she rode the high of her climax, I pulled away just long enough to pull down my pants and boxers and cover myself with a condom. When I slid inside her tight channel, she was so wet and still pulsing. I lowered my head against the area between her neck and shoulder and released a guttural moan.

"You always feel so good," I uttered. "I want to fuck you forever."

As soon as I heard that final word, I regretted it. Why say things that could never be?

"Yes," she cried.

I wished she meant it, but it only came out in the heat of passion.

Shoving that moment aside, I focused on the incredible sensation of rocking in and out of her lush body. She clung to me and released the most delicious sounds. I tilted to an angle that drove her wild, providing the friction she needed to chase that rising crescendo.

She bucked against me, tightening her limbs.

"Come for me, babe. I want to feel you come on my cock."

"Yes." She arched her body and came with a strangled cry.

The intense tightness around my shaft propelled me with her. I gripped her by her lush ass and slammed myself into her twice more before exploding with her into the void.

I held onto her for a long while after as we recovered, our hearts pounding and breath coming hard.

WE ATE BREAKFAST TOGETHER AND THEN SPENT A FEW HOURS doing our own things. As I hiked through the woods, the delicious high of our morning still electrifying my body, I thought about what would happen when she returned to school.

It was the end of us. That was the only way. What else could there be? She didn't want to be tethered to a damaged, isolated soul like me.

It would be the end of us.

To avoid dwelling on that and sinking into one of my dark moods, I tried to make the most of our short time together. New Year's Eve was in two days. Since Christmas had gone so well, maybe we should opt to do something low key together.

After a scrumptious breakfast-for-dinner meal that night with hearty huevos rancheros, we settled in front of the fireplace with steaming mugs of Mexican hot chocolate. Rosanna leaned against me as we stared at the crackling fire. Outside, the snow had melted from many of the tree branches, but several inches remained on the ground. That provided enough of a base for cross-country skiing. She hadn't come with me since Christmas day, saying she didn't want to slow me down, but I liked having her with me. I spent enough time alone in this cottage.

"It's almost New Year's Eve," I said. "What do you usually do?"

She exhaled. "Truthfully, they've all been pretty lackluster. My stepsisters have dragged me to parties during which time I thought how I'd rather be home. That's what I did last year— stayed home alone, reading a book, and watching the ball drop. Trust me, I was much happier that way."

"I can see that."

"What about you?" She cocked her head.

I chuckled. "I've spent too many of them the past ten years away from home. If I was on base, we'd go to someone's party and get stupid drunk. Not our finest moments."

"Okay, what was your best one?" she asked me.

I thought about it. "Probably the ones here with my family when I was younger. We'd go skiing during the day and then come back here, exhausted. We'd sit in front of the fire and watch the ball drop on TV."

"That sounds fantastic. My best ones were when my mother was alive. We'd order Chinese food and just be together."

The way she missed her mother made me feel for how I sometimes clashed with mine. Rosanna would do anything to have her mother back. I loved my mother with my entire being, but we were both stubborn and thought we knew what was best. Too alike.

Yet, my mother was the reason why Rosanna was here, so a point went to her. A big fat point.

Rosanna's gaze drifted off as she appeared to reminisce. She then turned to me with a meaningful glance. "Let's do it."

"Do what?"

"Go skiing on New Year's Eve."

"You want to?" I asked with surprise.

"Sure, why not? It sounds like fun."

It did have a certain appeal. We hadn't been out of the cottage much, and it might be something fun to do together. Besides, I wore a face mask when I skied, which didn't stand out as odd since many others did. I appreciated the break from the gawking at my scars.

"Okay, let's do it." I pulled out my phone to see if we could book tickets. "The two closest mountains are Killington and Pico. But there are others nearby."

"I don't think I'm ready to tackle Killington," she said. "I'm too rusty." She slapped her thighs. "Haven't tested out my ski legs in a couple of years."

"Cross-country didn't count?"

"No. A different kind of movement. I'm sure I'll be hurting after the first day skiing downhill. Have you gone yet?"

"Once at Killington."

"That means you've already broken in your ski legs." She bit her lower lip. "I bet you're an amazing skier, aren't you? A Navy SEAL who tackles the moguls and black diamonds."

I laughed. "Slightly guilty."

"What does that mean?"

"I *try* to tackle them. But sometimes it backfires, and they tackle me."

When Rosanna laughed, my heart warmed. She leaned against my chest again. I wished I could bottle up this moment and save it. Because no matter how badly I wanted to keep it forever, I knew it wouldn't last.

ROSANNA

"This was a fantastic idea," I gushed to Leo after we finished the second run on a green trail.

The mountain was covered with fresh snow, drawing out the crowds. Sounds of others zipping downhill or conversing surrounded us. The blue sky was perfect for visibility and picturesque views of other mountains in the distance. The air was crisp and cool. An occasional breeze kicked up some of the fluffy white snow, but it wasn't a gust that would have me bracing against the wind.

"Plenty of powder," Leo said, kicking some off his skis.

"I know people love the fluffy stuff, but the challenge sneaks up on you," I noted.

"I'll take it." He motioned to the sky. "Besides, it's a perfect bluebird day," Leo agreed.

His royal blue ski jacket and black ski pants were a stark contrast against the whiteness of the snow. A black helmet, goggles, and mask shielded much of his face, yet I sensed he was content. It was in the lines of his more relaxed stance. When we'd arrived at the mountain, his form was stiff and guarded, the same way it started whenever we entered a public space like a supermarket.

I liked seeing him like this. Fumbling to take off my gloves and then pull out my phone, I snapped a photo.

"Did you take a picture of me?" he asked.

"I did," I admitted.

He cocked his head. "Why?"

"You look happy. And I like seeing you happy."

And I wanted to capture a memory of this for when I returned to school. We hadn't talked about what would happen between us after I left, so I had to assume this was simply a fling. It would hurt to leave him, but I understood. He'd come to the cabin to isolate himself. Sure, he might be enjoying the hot sex each night—and sometimes in the day—as much as I had, but that didn't mean we had any sort of future. It would be smarter of me not to think like that to avoid getting hurt.

"Then I'm getting one of you," he added in a light tone.

"Oh jeez." I was probably a mess with my hair tousled by the wind beneath my helmet.

Before I could make any adjustments such as smoothing my hair, he snapped some photos.

"Let's get a selfie with the mountains behind us," I suggested.

He skied over to me and aligned his skies besides mine. I leaned my helmet head onto his shoulder. He took some photos and showed them to me.

He chuckled. "We look like motorcycle ninjas."

"True." I laughed. With our faces covered, it looked that way, but the goggles didn't conceal the glimmer in our eyes. "But we look happy."

Leo stared at the screen. "We do indeed." After a few seconds, he asked, "Ready to try a blue?"

"I think so." It had been a few years since I'd gone skiing, so I'd eased into it on the easier trails, which also let me get to the rental skis. My form might still be rusty, but I'd felt more confident with each run.

Of course, the blue trails were a breeze for Leo. He skied

down without any trouble, stopping at cross-trails to make sure we didn't lose each other.

By the end of the morning, we'd worked up to the black diamonds. I was cautious, but since the snow was fluffy, it wouldn't be like skiing over ice patches. That freaked me out. The sound of skies scraping against ice rang as a warning. At least if I fell on one of these, it would be a softer landing than falling on ice.

We paused for a quick and early lunch in the cafeteria with two bowls of clam chowder in a bread bowl. The heat of the hearty broth soothed the chill from outdoors, and the tang of clams and spices was delicious on my tongue.

"This is so much fun," I said to Leo.

"Looks like we're not the only ones who thought of coming here." He motioned around us. Several people, including many families, filled up the lodge.

"True."

"You're doing great," he praised. "How are you feeling?"

"Tired but this break helps."

"Do you want to go back out after lunch or head home?"

Home. That word sent a shiver of delight through me.

"I think I can go out some more."

"That's my girl," he praised with a proud glint in his eyes.

Those words affected me even more so, even if he didn't mean anything by it.

We returned to the slopes after lunch. I tried a couple of the glades at a slow speed but opted to take a break when Leo suggested the moguls.

"No, thank you." I laughed. "It would take me the rest of the afternoon to work up the courage to get down them."

"We can do something else," he said.

"No, go ahead. I'm ready for a rest, anyway." I motioned for him to head to the chair lifts.

While we were separated, I thought about the night ahead,

cozying up with Leo in front of the fireplace while we rang in the new year. We could snuggle with a beverage while we counted down to midnight and then celebrate with a kiss. I couldn't think of a more perfect ending to a wonderful day.

Never would I have thought the opportunity of coming here to work in the mountains would turn out this way, especially after the cool introduction from Leo. As he'd slowly warmed up to me and showed his gentler side, I'd started to fall for him.

What did that mean when my time here was up?

I heaved out a sigh. Nothing. We hadn't talked about us as having any sort of relationship. It was safer for me to think of this as living in the moment. Leo had given me no reason to think our little affair would continue.

Although I admired him, maybe it was foolish. Underneath it all, he could have been just as much as a commitment-phobe as every other guy I'd dated in college. Guys wanted one thing. If I thought otherwise, I might be setting myself up for a fall.

I pushed that thought aside when I met up with Leo again for some more runs. No need to put a damper on a wonderful day by ruminating about things that may or may not happen. Why not live in the moment and enjoy what we had while we had it?

"READY TO CALL IT A DAY?" LEO ASKED ME LATER THAT afternoon.

"Oh yes," I replied. "Not only am I cold but beat. Skiing kicked my butt today."

As he removed his skis and leaned them onto the rack, he said, "You did great, especially for someone who hasn't skied for a couple of years."

After I removed mine, Leo placed his hand on my lower back, and we headed inside the lodge. Music reached us through the bustle. A band had started playing, drawing people into the pub. We removed our helmets, face masks, and gloves.

"Looks like après-ski time has started," he pointed out.

"Nice. Let's go there."

We removed our ski boots and pants, and I returned my gear to the rental shop. Then we headed over to the pub and sat at a high-top. My feet screamed in relief at having a break from the tight fit of the ski boots. A server brought over glasses of ice water and a bowl of popcorn.

"Welcome. What can I get you?"

I glanced at the drink menu, searching for the hot drinks. "I'd love an Irish coffee."

"Sounds good. Make that two," Leo added.

While she went to get our drinks, we scoured the rest of the menu.

"What are you in the mood for?" Leo asked me.

I grinned. "I'm still full from the chowder. Want to share nachos?"

"Good choice," he agreed with a nod.

It turned out the heaping plate of tortilla chips, salsa, beans, guacamole, and cheese was more than enough as we didn't even finish the plate. Combined with the rich coffee drinks, I think I'd restored some of the calories I'd burned off while skiing.

"I can't move." When I leaned back in the chair, I placed my hand on my stomach. "I don't know if it's from skiing or the nachos."

He nodded. "You did great out there. Ready to head home?"

Home. I loved the sound of that. "Yes."

After he paid, we gathered our gear and headed out of the pub.

"Shit," Leo muttered under his breath.

"What's wrong?" I asked.

"My ex-girlfriend is headed this way."

CHAPTER 13

LEO

$\mathcal{J}$ searched for a way to slip away before Eva spotted us. The men's room and store were ahead, but she'd already passed it, so it didn't do much good. We were stuck in the hallway walking toward each other.

"Turn around," I told Rosanna out of desperation.

"What?" she asked in an incredulous tone.

I turned toward the wall, feigning interest in a flyer on the wall. "Come with me." I then headed in the opposite direction.

A family grumbled as they had to veer around me with all their gear.

"Leo?"

Damn. It was Eva. Too late.

I cocked my head just enough to glance at her while trying to hide my scarred side.

"Hi, Eva." I forced a friendly tone but could hear how it sounded forced. "How are you?"

"Great. I haven't seen you in a long time." We were heading

in the same direction now, which was even worse. She stopped walking and turned to me. Her gaze traveled to my scar.

Insecurities flared as I was on display. If I'd put my ski mask back on already, I could have avoided this uncomfortable encounter. Eva knew me when I was young and whole. Now I was scarred and broken—a visual confirmation that she'd made the right choice in leaving me.

She stared at me as if waiting, and I realized she'd asked a question.

"What was that?"

"I asked how you've been."

"Oh, fine, fine," I stammered and glanced at Rosanna. Realizing my rudeness, I stumbled, "This is Rosanna." My caretaker? Lover? I didn't have a clue about how to introduce her. "Rosanna, this is Eva."

They exchanged greetings. How could I get out of this conversation? I'd rather climb to the top of the mountain barefoot in the snow than deal with this uncomfortable situation.

"Great day for skiing, isn't it?" Eva said.

"Yes." My muscles burned with tension, and my skin stretched tightly over them.

"Are you still in the Navy?"

I shook my head. "No," I barked.

Rosanna glanced at me. Was that a subtle warning about my tone?

"I got out earlier this year."

"And you're back living here?"

"For now." Jeez, had I never had a conversation before? Why not just grunt and groan like a beast? I searched my addled brain for manners. "How about you?"

"I never left." A man and two school-aged kids approached. She turned to them. "Justin, this is an old friend, Leo." Then to me, she said, "Leo, this is my husband, Justin, and our kids, Tori and Tommy."

I grumbled pleasantries. Of course, she got married to some good-looking dude, and they had the perfect family. She talked about where they were staying for a family ski vacation. They had to be well off. Skiing was expensive. Skiing with an entire family slope side during an entire peak week would be crazy so.

That was one of the things that had bothered me when we dated—she was into spending money, especially mine.

"We're going to get something to eat," she said. "Good seeing you. Happy New Year!"

Once they left, my heart pounded.

"Are you okay, Leo?" Rosanna asked, her tone concerned.

"I'm fine," I lied.

"You seem a little shaken," she pointed out.

True. Seeing Eva after all this time rattled me, reminding me of who I once was before the world kicked the shit out of me.

Eva was right to have ended things. She would have hated the lifestyle that I'd lived during the past decade. She was much better off with a guy like Justin who gave her the perfect family and lavish ski vacations, instead of being stuck with someone who was now broken and scarred.

I wasn't fit to be in a relationship then and especially not now. I glanced at Rosanna.

Was Rosanna only into me for the same reason—my family's money?

Concern filled her eyes. "Did she mean something to you?"

Rosanna was different. She was sweet and caring.

I gulped. "A long, long time ago. She dumped me after I enlisted."

"Oh." Rosanna nodded with an understanding expression. "It must have been difficult to see her."

"I haven't since we broke up."

"Is there anything I can do?"

Seeing Eva had hit me like an avalanche. Had I been fooling myself these past few days thinking that things could be different with Rosanna? That we had a chance? That she was different, and she could be with someone like me?

Was I seeing what I wanted to see? It could all be wishful thinking—just like thinking we might be able to build something real and lasting. It wasn't possible. She was only here for a short period and had her reasons, none of which had to do with me. This job offered her an escape from her family and a place to work on her novel while giving her a paycheck. A few orgasms here and there were a bonus, right? Maybe I'd been reading her wrong the entire time due to my loneliness.

"No," I finally barked.

Dealing with me was the unfortunate price she had to pay. Whatever I thought had been building between us had to have been fabricated in my head. Sleeping with me might be out of pity. It couldn't be out of anything more.

Because I was the beast.

And no one could love a monster.

ROSANNA

Leo was quiet during the drive home after the ski trip. Although we watched some of the New Year's celebration on television with champagne cocktails, he said he was tired.

"I think I'm going to head upstairs. Spend some time in my studio and then go to bed. I'll see you in the morning."

Ouch. That was a clear *don't-come-to-my-room-tonight.* "Okay," I said with a forced smile. "Happy New Year."

"Happy New Year." He said it without enthusiasm and then took the stairs two at a time.

Was he that eager to get away from me? I turned to the television and took a sip of my champagne. So much for the midnight kiss.

· · ·

THE QUIET CONTINUED THE NEXT MORNING. HE WASN'T AROUND for much of the day. I didn't know if he'd gone out or was hiding in his studio. Was he avoiding me?

No, I was just being sensitive. After all, this was how he was. He spent time by himself. Just because we'd had sex didn't mean we had to spend every moment together. I attempted to carry on like nothing happened and made a beef stew for dinner.

He climbed down from upstairs while it was cooking. Had he been here all along?

"Hope you're hungry," I said. "I made a ton of beef stew."

He grunted. "Sure."

During dinner, he replied to my questions, but the conversations weren't as lively as they had been.

After we cleaned up, I suggested, "Movie or game tonight?"

"Actually, I'm a little burnt out from all this activity. I could use some time on my own to decompress."

"Oh, okay," I said, trying not to take it personally. After all, he was used to spending all his time alone, and he'd been spending much of the past week with me. Not only had I pushed him out of his comfort zone with the holiday celebrations, but that ski trip must have taken a lot out of him.

He avoided me for much of the next day as well. I tried to focus on my own projects, but at the back of my mind, something bothered me. Was sleeping with him a mistake?

I thought Leo was different. I thought he was better than that. Was I wrong?

Regardless, no matter how hot the sex was, it had to have been a mistake because now he was avoiding me. And it all started after the ski trip, after he'd run into his ex.

Did he still have feelings for her?

I couldn't think of any other explanation. And since Leo only spoke in clipped answers or groans when I tried to talk to him, it wasn't likely he'd confide in me.

Since I didn't know what to make of it, I called Daniel from my room. After I explained the situation, he winced.

"Ouch." He followed that with a hissing sound.

My muscles tensed. I adjusted my position on the bed. "What?"

"It doesn't sound good."

"I know it doesn't sound good. That's why I'm calling you. What do you think?"

He smacked his lips together. "Guys are jerks, Rosanna. They just want one thing."

"Leo's not a jerk," I defended. Okay, maybe he was in the beginning, but he'd changed so much since then.

Or had he?

"Don't get too hung up on him," Daniel warned. "Could he still have a thing for her?"

I sagged. That's what I was afraid of. "I don't know. What would you do if you were me?"

Daniel nudged his chin up. "I'd want to know. I'd ask him straight out about it. None of this dancing around, speculating bullshit. Who has time for that?"

I nodded slowly. "Yeah, you're right."

The next night at dinner, I couldn't take it any longer. I'd cooked chicken ziti broccoli and served it with a chilled white wine. Leo praised it as delicious, the way he often did, but he was still distant.

"What's going on, Leo?"

His gaze brushed over me. "What do you mean?"

"You've been avoiding me the past few days, since the ski trip. What happened?"

"Nothing." He rolled one shoulder and avoided my gaze.

"Bullshit."

He stared at me with surprise.

"Is it your ex?"

He stabbed the pasta so quickly, I knew I hit on something.

"What about her?"

"Do you still have feelings for her?"

He blinked at me with an incredulous expression. "Are you serious?"

"I am."

"No, of course not." He resumed eating. "By the way, this is really good."

He'd already said that. Okay, so he was changing the subject and denying it had anything to do with her. Then what was it? What else could have darkened his mood so abruptly? His words were one thing but actions another. He hadn't touched me since we'd returned from that trip.

I dropped the subject, and I tried again not to take it personally.

Remember why you're here. Right, it damn well wasn't to hook up with a guy, especially one who was going to play games with me. If he didn't want anything to do with me, fine. I wasn't going to chase him. If he wanted his distance, so be it. I didn't need him and had plenty to do to keep me occupied while I finished out my time here.

While he spent the next couple of days outside or in the studio, I worked on my projects. I sketched out ideas for what I could write about for my final project. I read and watched movies, jotting bits that inspired me. I wrote notes for characters and descriptions of settings. I played with ideas for plots and conflicts. I thought of people I met and noted traits, both positive and negative, that could come in handy when I created characters.

One of my character sketches was on Leo. He was so complex and so interesting to me, even his dark moods. What went on in his head? Why could he be so sweet and considerate and yet so aloof and distant? Maybe by writing things down, I'd get a better idea of the man I was temporarily living with.

That worked for a day until the silence got to me. At dinner that night, I asked, "What are you doing up in your studio?"

"Painting."

A one-word answer with no details. Okay. "What are you painting?"

"Paintings." He arched a brow. "You know, the old verb and noun word play."

He flashed a lopsided grin, and I saw a glimpse of the man I'd started falling for, the man who'd teased me about words when he kicked my butt Scrabble. Maybe that was a way to break through?

"Are you up for a game tonight? I need a rematch for Scrabble."

He glanced away for several seconds before replying, "Sure."

While he set up the game, I made some hot cocoa. He put on an alternative rock playlist at low volume in the background.

While we played, I tried to start conversations. He'd reply but wouldn't offer more. This discussion was definitely one-sided. He'd talk about the different plays of the game but not much else. The silences between each play grew louder and more awkward despite the music playing.

I was losing Leo, and I wasn't sure why.

Maybe I never even had him.

CHAPTER 14

LEO

aving Rosanna so close was torment. I'd agreed to play the game as I could see how I was hurting her. But it was a bad idea. How could I be around her and not want to touch her? The temptation to lean closer and inhale the scent of her shampoo or run my fingers through her silky hair would be too strong. I couldn't sit near her and not want to trail my fingers over her soft skin.

Her lips were there, so full and tempting. How could I sit across from her each night at dinner and not be captivated by them? How could I suppress the urge to trace her tempting curves, remembering how she responded to my touch?

My staying away was for her own good. The more distance and doors between us, the less likely I'd be tempted by the urges to be with her. I'd killed hour after hour walking in the woods or painting in my studio.

But tonight, I agreed to sit with her and play Scrabble. And it might have been a mistake.

"What is it, Leo?" she asked me.

I stared at her. "What?"

"You look…" She pursed her lips as if searching for the word. "Disturbed."

That was one way to put it. Ever since the ski trip, the darkness had been taking hold. I knew I wasn't good enough for Rosanna. She could do so much better than me.

Still, she tried and tried to reach out to me. That was part of the goodness of her soul, which drew me to her. When she'd asked if I still had feelings for Eva, I assured her that I didn't. But I didn't admit that Eva was the catalyst to remind me why I should pull away.

"I'm fine," I lied.

Asking Rosanna to stay was the worst thing I could have done to her. She could have found a job and a living arrangement by now. But now it was too late. I couldn't ask her to leave and scramble to find something else. We'd just have to get through the next couple of weeks of living together.

So, I kept my distance despite every part of me wanting to go to her. Why bother when this couldn't go anywhere, anyway? She'd go back to school, and I'd fester here. I couldn't bring her anything but darkness and mood swings, catapulting her into my pain.

She cocked her head. "Did I do something to turn you off?"

"Turn me off?" I repeated with incredulity. "Absolutely not."

"Then why have you been avoiding me?"

Her eyes were so full of pain, I cursed myself. I'd do anything to take that way.

"Because I'm not right for you. You burn with this—" I gestured, turning my palm, as I searched for the word— "brightness. Vivacity." I pointed to my chest. "Me, I'm trapped in darkness. And I don't want to snuff out your light."

"Leo…" She exhaled with a soft sigh. "We all have darkness.

And we all have light." She leaned closer to me and cupped my scarred cheek. "Even you."

With her mere inches away, I struggled against every urge to touch her. Her scent surrounded and calmed me.

"I don't want to hurt you," I said. "And I don't know how not to do so."

She raised her chin a notch. "Staying away from me is what hurts. And maybe for you as well?"

Hell, she was right. And she was too close. Too tempting. Her mouth was right there.

I should run. I should hide in my studio or go out and walk all night until the urge to be with her lessened.

But I didn't want to leave her. My mind and body clashed, warring with the need for her and to shield us both from pain. The draw to her won.

I leaned closer and brushed my lips against hers. The moment we touched ignited a fierce longing in me, one I'd been trying to suppress for days.

"Rosanna," I whispered against her ear.

She responded with a low, needy whimper. Desire kindled, soon erupting into full-blown flames as we grasped at each other. I pulled off her shirt and then mine, tossing both to the floor, before we came together once more in a feverish kiss. I pressed my body against hers, our bare skin touching, and leaned her back on the sofa.

Desperate to be inside her once again and ready to claim her right there, I managed to pull my mouth away a fraction to growl, "Upstairs."

I wanted more room to explore the canvas of her beautiful body. As we moved up to my room, we lost more clothing. By the time I lay her on the bed, she was only in a pair of tiny black panties. I only had my boxers left. She stared up at me from hooded eyes, the desire was back in her gaze. The look I craved, the look I missed. The one I feared I'd snuffed out.

I climbed on top of her and kissed her from her face and all down her torso. I flicked my tongue around her nipples and moaned as I took each breast in my mouth. What kind of fool was I to resist this goddess who wanted me for some mysterious reason?

"Leo." My name fell from her lips on a sigh.

Yes, I needed more of that. I wanted to make her feel nothing but pleasure.

I moved down her body, kissing and teasing her. When I brushed feather-light kisses up her thighs, she squirmed on the sheets. I rose, deliberately drawing out the anticipation until she fisted the sheets.

"Please," she begged.

I wouldn't torment either of us any longer. When I tasted her sweet core, she released a breathy moan. Why had I stayed away from her these past few days? I wanted her, needed her, and she appeared to want the same from me.

I savored her addictive tang, drawing out her pleasure as our excitement rose. She writhed on the sheets, whispering my name in a strangled plea. I brought her higher and higher, and she arched her body off the bed. Then her muscles tightened, and she crashed with a desperate cry.

As I let her come down from her high, my cock throbbed. I needed to be inside her. With a final kiss, I pulled away to find a condom. Those seconds of waiting as I fumbled to put one on were brutal.

"Hurry," she pleaded and reached for me. "I need you."

"I need you, too," I replied and climbed on top of her.

When I slid inside her slick, velvet tightness, a low moan rumbled from deep within my core. "Fuck, you feel so good," I rumbled.

I drove in deeper and harder. She matched my rhythm from below, meeting my quickening pace. With how incredible this felt, I wouldn't last long.

"Turn over," I directed.

While she adjusted her position, I took a few seconds to regain some control. But once I entered her from behind, the desire took over. I pounded into her as if possessed, my beastly side coming through as she yelped and gasped and clutched the sheets.

I reached around and found her sensitive bud, stroking as I drove in from behind. She bucked against me, wilder than ever. I sensed her getting closer.

When she crashed, she cried out my name, drawing me over the edge with her. I exploded with a guttural moan and then fell forward, resting my head against her back.

We pulled apart and recovered, panting side by side. I then spooned her from behind and held her. But for how long? Soon, she'd leave the cottage and go back to her life.

Soon, she'd leave me, and I'd be here with alone with my darkness.

ROSANNA

After that magical night, I thought things would be better this morning. But Leo was gone.

He wasn't in his bed. He wasn't downstairs. He didn't leave a note.

What the hell? I thought we'd bridged whatever distance that had developed between us. That had to be wrong. Because there was no sign of him this morning.

Or was I going crazy?

In the shower, I scrubbed my hair with vigor. Why was he being like this?

The only explanation that made sense had to do with the timeline. Leo saw his ex on the ski trip. He retreated soon after. Seeing her must have brought back feelings; it must have reminded him of what they had. Had he ever gotten over her?

Despite his denial, the answer was clear in his actions. No.

I groaned as I rinsed the shampoo out of my hair. What a fool I was to think last night meant anything. Sure, he slept with me because he was a guy and that's what guys wanted. When he woke up today, he regretted it and took off.

Hadn't I learned anything in college? Guys only wanted one thing. Nothing more. No commitments. I snorted. I'd been deluding myself by thinking Leo was different.

I quickly finished up and got dressed. As I brushed my hair, I scolded myself not to be naïve anymore. I was here for a job, nothing more. Definitely not a relationship that would go nowhere.

When Leo came back from wherever he was, I'd make that clear.

Morning lengthened into afternoon and still no sign of Leo. I made myself a roast beef and brie sandwich with pickles and chips for lunch, half-expecting him to come through the door. Maybe he'd ask me to make one for him. I'd do so but would remain aloof. If he wanted to be distant, so could I. What I wasn't going to do was throw myself at him any longer.

I read near the fireplace for an hour and then dashed up to the bathroom. When I glanced down to the open door to his bedroom, a pang of loss tumbled through me. But then my gaze fixed on the closed door beside it—his studio.

Could he be in there?

I took a few hesitant steps down the hall. Why was I being so cautious? I wasn't sure. Maybe it was because he didn't want me to go in there.

Continuing, I stopped before it and listened. No music or any sound indicating he was in there.

I raised my hand and paused for a few seconds. "Leo?" I knocked on the door.

No answer.

I knocked once more. "Are you in there?"

Still nothing.

What was he hiding in there?

Curiosity rose.

I put my hand on the knob. The metal was cool on my hand. My pulse raced. I knew this was wrong but couldn't stop myself. What was his secret? Was it a shrine to his ex and his love for her? Was he secretly some serial killer, and I'd step into some torture chamber?

No, I didn't seriously think either of those were true, but what if there was something in there, something dangerous, that he was keeping from me? After all, I was staying with him under the same roof. I should be allowed to investigate to ensure that both he and I were safe.

Or what if he was a danger to himself?

With the way his mood had darkened, it wasn't something I could easily dismiss. He was hurting about something. Was it enough to push him over the edge?

I thought of my mother and what had happened to her. My heart beat faster. I remembered how I'd seen her in bed, looking like she was asleep. But she was lifeless. My father's anguished howls had confirmed the devastating truth. She was gone.

I had suspicions about what had happened but never told anyone. Why bother? It wouldn't change the fact that she was gone and would have only brought my father more pain. He'd attempted to pull himself together and start a new life with a new family. Even if I didn't think he chose well, he seemed happy enough.

But if anyone had taken the time to ask my mother if she was okay, would it have changed the outcome?

This was a leap and a giant one. But what had happened to my mother was tragic enough that even a sliver of that possibility of the same thing happening to Leo was enough to spur me on. Didn't I owe it to his mother as well? If anything happened to him...

Even if he hated me for it, I had to make sure he was okay.

I put my hand on the doorknob and turned it. It was probably locked, anyway.

Stop. You made a promise.

I did. But I'd also created reasons why I had to break the promise.

They won. I pushed the door. To my surprise, it wasn't locked. I opened it a few inches and peeked inside. Paintings. Many were mounted on the limited wall space. An empty easel with paints was set before a window.

My mouth dropped open. That wasn't what I expected. He'd told me he painted up here but with the privacy, I figured he was hiding some deep, dark secret. This is what he wanted to keep from me? Why? The paintings were beautiful, of mountains and forests and familiar Vermont landscapes.

I stepped deeper inside the room and gasped. The paintings turned abruptly dark. The landscapes were gone, replaced by abstract pieces. Lots of angry reds and stark black. Many mouths open in anguish, screaming in agony. Battlefields. My gaze scanned over canvas after canvas of vivid horror. Chaos. Destruction. Death.

Oh God. My hand fluttered to my mouth. What had Leo gone through? It must have been so terrible to endure.

This was how he dealt with his pain. Compassion struck hard, and my hand lowered to my chest. I felt so much for him.

"What are you doing?"

The clipped, pained voice startled me, and I jumped back, bumping into a hard chest.

I turned and stared into his furious gaze. "Leo."

"I asked you not to come in here." His voice was colder than the icicles frozen against the window.

"I know but—but I was worried."

He pointed at me, his blue eyes flashing with accusation. "You lied to me, Rosanna. Betrayed me."

"No." I stepped back. "I—I—I just wanted to make sure you were okay."

"By snooping?" he arched his brows.

"No." Technically, he was right. "Well, yes." I lowered my head in shame. "I'm sorry."

"Now you know my secret," he spat. "I'm not just a freak on the outside but hideous inside as well."

"Leo, that's not true." I stepped toward him. "This is exactly what I was talking about when I suggested writing to process your feelings. You found another way through painting." I moved my hand toward his chest. "I think that's wonderful."

"Wonderful?" He snorted and stepped back. "You think my pain is wonderful?"

"No, of course not. That's not what I mean."

He turned his head, and I couldn't see his face. "How would you like it if I went through your stuff? Stuff you didn't want other people to see?"

He turned and left the room. Where was he going?

"Leo." I followed his large strides down the hall. He pushed my bedroom door open.

My heart pounded in my ears. "What are you doing?"

My laptop was on top of the bed. He grabbed it and opened it.

"Leo, stop," I pleaded.

If he saw what I wrote… My throat tightened.

He stared at the screen, eyes widening. When he raised his gaze to meet mine, his eyes were narrowed to slits.

"You've been writing about me."

"No." I stepped forward and attempt to reach for my laptop.

He yanked it away and continued reading. "Is that why you came here?" His blue eyes darkened with shadows. "I suspected you'd spy on me for my mother. But for your own personal gain?"

Shame swelled inside, threatening to swallow me. I bit my lower lip. "It's not like that. Please, let me explain."

He closed his eyes. When he reopened them, they were full of so much anguish, I wished I could do anything to take it away. "You don't need to explain." His expression turned hard and his voice cold, unrecognizable. "I've seen enough." He pressed some keys and then turned the screen to face me. The document was blank. He saved and closed it, deleting all my work.

My mouth dropped open. "Why did you do that? You deleted everything I've worked on since I was here." All the notes, all the character sketches, all the plot point—gone.

"Good!" He sneered. "I'm not your subject. You can't turn my pain into material for your book."

I blinked at him. "I would never do that. It was just some brainstorming exercises."

"I don't care what it was. You still exploited me for your own interests."

"Leo," I attempted to reason through the throbbing confusion. "Let's go downstairs and talk about this."

He turned away with disgust. "I was a fool to think there was anything between us. After all, you're only here for a job." His lips curled downward. "Have you been spying on me for my mother and giving her reports as well?"

"No, of course not."

He sneered. "And not only did you get paid, but you got off as well." He gestured with an abrupt wave. "Why not throw in a few orgasms, right?"

I winced at the callous picture he painted of me. "It wasn't like that at all." I struggled to hold in the tears.

He faced me again, eyes vivid with fury. "I've heard enough." He pointed down the stairs. "Do me a favor, Rosanna."

"What?"

"Get out of my house and leave me the fuck alone."

CHAPTER 15

LEO

J should've known it was going too well. That none of
it was real.

I pounded out my frustration after Rosanna left the cottage
by chopping wood for the fireplace. Swing, slam. Satisfaction at
seeing the wood split in two pierced through the ache gnawing
at me inside.

Swing, slam. I'd gone on a long walk this morning after
being with her last night, wrestling with myself to see if there
was any conceivable way that we could make this work. When I
returned to my cottage, I planned to talk to her, to see what she
wanted.

To know if she wanted me after her time here was over.

Swing, slam. Seeing her invade my studio, my personal
space, after I'd specifically asked her not to do so was just the tip
of the betrayal. She made a promise and broke it. I should have
known better than to trust her. After all, she was just a stranger.

Then to read what she'd written on her laptop was the sharpened blade that scissored my heart.

She was writing about me. The reclusive vet scarred by war. Was that her intention when coming here? To find a subject she could write about? Or was that something she seized as an opportunity?

Either way, she spied on me. Lied to me. Used my agony as creative fodder.

I should've known that none of this was real. How could it be? She was only here for such a short time. By sending her away earlier, it avoided the inevitable—a painful, awkward goodbye. Perhaps it worked out better this way. No one felt forced to speak sentiments about seeing each other again soon or other declarations of things that would never be. She'd go back to living her life, and I'd go back to mine. Here. Alone.

Away from people. People hurt you when they left. And they always left in the end. I pushed Rosanna away before she rejected me. We didn't have a future—we couldn't—so it was better we ended it now.

After I was panting and sweating from chopping more wood than I needed, I returned inside. The cabin was empty. Quiet. Too quiet.

I put a suggested playlist on and poured myself a glass of whiskey. It wasn't often I drank the harder stuff, but all I wanted was oblivion. I stared at the trees outside, my gaze lost in the shadows while I listened to music and tried not to think.

That's all I did. Think.

A familiar song came on, Toto's "Rosanna." My muscles hardened. Blood rushed through my veins. What the fuck, universe? Was it hellbent on tormenting me? Bloody perfect.

I grabbed the small speaker and tossed it at the stone above the fireplace. It fell to the ground silent and broken.

I picked up my phone and raised my arm, ready to toss that as well. Common sense prevailed. I deleted the song from my favorites instead. It wasn't as satisfactory as splitting wood or smashing speakers, but still provided a hint of relief.

I took the stairs two at a time and entered my studio. I didn't let anybody in there for a reason. The darkness in my mind, all those horrible memories, lay exposed on the canvas. Anyone who saw those violent images would judge me in some way. They'd think I was too damaged. They might decide I needed more help. More therapy. More talking. More and more and more.

Therapists might consider me too screwed up to even be part of society anymore. Maybe they'd think it was safer to lock me up. After all, anyone who painted such horrific scenes had to have some serious mental issues, right?

People wanted you to paint happy scenes. Picturesque landscapes. Portraits. Not focus on the darkness. Not to deal with the nightmares that wouldn't leave your head. And you hoped—somehow you hoped—getting them out on the canvas would mean they'd leave you alone.

Seeing Eva when we were skiing should've woken me up sooner. It wasn't just a reality slap, it was a pugil stick to the gut. I should have ended things with Rosanna that night.

My ex now had the perfect life she wanted, the one she couldn't have with me. A husband who took care of her and their beautiful children. Who took them on expensive ski vacations. Who provided so there was never a need for anything.

Not someone who was scarred enough that young kids would stare when he went out in public. Adults would look and try not to gape, but the speculation was clear on their faces. The I-wonder-what-happened look I'd seen a thousand times.

Not someone who'd put a damper on family photos with his awful scar unless they were Photoshopped—and then if they were, it would be a reminder of the stark difference between a picture-perfect life and reality.

I didn't belong in family portraits. The only story that my

photo could tell was that something bad had happened. Something horrific.

Rosanna deserved a good man. Someone who could give her the perfect life with the perfect Christmas family photo. That was something I could never give her.

After all, I was here in the cottage so my family wouldn't have to put up with my dark moods during the holidays. They wanted to celebrate and be happy.

Funny how Rosanna had coaxed me to do so. I thought it had been wonderful. But in the end, it was just a farce. The ornaments and tinsels on the tree were temporary. The bright star perched on top of it, a short-lived glow. Once I unplugged the lights, the darkness returned.

Like it did now.

ROSANNA

"He kicked you out?" Daniel's mouth widened like he'd seen a ghost.

Two days and two bus trips later, I sat in his parent's house in New Jersey.

"Yes." I squirmed on the sofa in the family room. "I don't exactly blame him. What I did was wrong."

I'd given Daniel a brief overview when I'd called him yesterday and asked if I could stay with him after all. He picked me up at the train station today and brought me to his parents' large house in a New Jersey suburb. Fortunately, his parents were at work, so I didn't have to force a cheerful demeanor around them yet.

Now that Daniel and I were here, I curled up under a colorful crocheted afghan and gave him an overview, omitting the details about the paintings and how he'd deleted my writing. If there was one thing I'd discovered from Leo's outburst, it was how he thought I'd violated his privacy. I didn't want to make things even worse by revealing personal details.

"That doesn't mean he can throw you out on your ass in the middle of a Vermont winter." Daniel pursed his lips and crossed his arms.

"He thinks I betrayed him." I sighed and slumped into the cushions. "Maybe he's right. But I didn't do so intentionally."

Daniel's brows furrowed. "Did you talk to him about it?"

"I tried." I bit my lower lip. "He was so hurt and angry and didn't want to listen."

Daniel leaned back in the chair, ran one hand through his surfer-style, floppy blond hair, and crossed one leg over his thigh. "Let me get this straight. First, he didn't want you there and wanted you to leave. Then, he suggested a three-day trial. After that, he asked you to stay the entire duration. Things got hot between you, but then exploded, and he kicked you out."

There were plenty more nuances and details and hot or tender moments in between. I sighed. "That's the gist of it."

His expression turned serious. "How do you feel about it all?"

I snorted. "Good question."

"Meaning?"

"I'm still processing everything."

"Did you develop feelings for him?" Daniel asked in a sympathetic tone.

I pressed my lips together. A part of me wanted to shield myself from this heartache and say no. That was bullshit, purely defensive.

Closing my eyes, I pictured Leo's face. How bright his blue eyes would glint when he was happy. How dark they'd gotten when I'd hurt him. "Yes."

Daniel brought his fingertips to his lips and then lowered his hands. "Did he develop feelings for you?"

I reopened my eyes. "I thought so, but that whole encounter with his ex makes me question that."

"This is tricky," Daniel declared. "When someone you care about hurts you, even if it's unintentional, its brutal."

I winced and covered my heart. "Thanks for making me feel better."

"I'm getting there," Daniel said. "The way I see it is that you have two choices. It starts with a question: Do you want to resolve things with him?"

I glanced outside the picture window while I considered the question. There was less snow down here than we'd had up in Vermont but still enough to leave a coating on the trees. Whereas up there, I'd look onto the snowy forests, here some trees lined the residential road, with houses beyond it.

"What's the point?" I turned to Daniel. "I'm going back to school next week. We live in different states. He doesn't want anything to do with me."

"You can't be sure of that. But I'm not asking about what he wants," Daniel added. "I'm asking what *you* want."

The truth was I hated the way we'd left things. How had something that had felt magical turned so ugly?

"I do," I admitted. "I don't want us to leave things the way they were."

He nodded and brought his fingertips beneath his chin. "It sounds to me like you have two clear options: try to talk to him about what happened or walk away with regret."

I grimaced. "Ouch."

"Exactly."

"How am I supposed to fix things if he won't talk to me?"

Daniel stood and walked over to me. He nudged my knee. "You're a writer. I'm sure you can find another way." Then he winked. "What's your choice comfort food or beverage right now? Ice cream, tea, or mudslides?"

The corner of my lips curled upward. "Since I'm going to be here for the rest of the week, will I get all three?"

He grinned. "Absolutely."

"You're the best. How about some soothing tea to start?"

"You got it." He walked into the kitchen, leaving me alone to think.

Over the next few days, Daniel helped distract me from my misery with his sunny disposition. He showed me some of his favorite spots back home, from where to get the best ice cream, even though it was in the middle of winter, to where he played hockey at the ice-skating rink. We went one night and skated, him expertly and me clinging to his arm awkwardly until I took refuge on the bench with a hot cocoa.

Being here with a friend was better than being somewhere alone to wallow, but it didn't take away my thoughts at night. That's when the rumination returned. I rewrote the last day at the cottage, envisioning other ways I could have handled it. Better ways.

On my last day in New Jersey, I decided to do something about it. One night when I couldn't sleep, I took Daniel's words to heart. I could write to Leo. There was no guarantee he would read it. He might detest me for what I'd done, but I had to explain and apologize, so I wouldn't spend night after night writhing in remorse.

CHAPTER 16

LEO

"*L*eo, what a surprise!" My mother threw her arms around me. "We weren't expecting you."

Her familiar floral perfume wrapped around me, one she'd worn since I was young.

"I decided to come after all." The holidays were over, and I didn't have to put on a fake smile to not bring everyone down. Actually, I was seeking a distraction. I had to get out of the cottage and all the memories of being there with Rosanna.

When my mother pulled back, she drew her dark brows together tightly. "What happened with Rosanna?"

I ground my teeth enough to hear them scrape. "Nothing."

"She told me you'd asked her to leave and that she was leaving the cottage. And that you'd paid for the rest of the stay so not to send her anything else. Is this all true?"

"Yes." My mother wasn't going to make this easy, was she?

"I thought you two were getting along so well?" She sighed. "Especially with celebrating Christmas together."

No way was I going to admit to my mother how I'd thrown Rosanna out—if she hadn't already told her. That didn't appear to be the case as my mother would have slapped me upside the head by now.

"I gave it a go, but there was no need to continue the arrangement. You didn't want me alone for the holidays, and I wasn't." When my mother fixed her probing gaze on me, I added, "Don't worry, I paid out the remainder of the contract and then some for her trouble."

My mother put her hands on her hips. "That's not what I'm concerned about. What happened?"

I exhaled. "Mom, are you happy that I'm here or not?"

"Of course I'm happy." She huffed. "But—"

"No buts," I cut her off. "I'm here to visit you for a few days. I thought you'd be pleased."

My mother stared at me and clucked her tongue. She appeared ready to question me some more but closed her mouth as if she thought better of it. "Yes, I'm glad you're here."

Over the next few days, I tried to distract myself from thinking of Rosanna. My mother brought her up in conversations a few times, asking what we did, and I avoided answering. I'd steer the discussion to other things, like food or family or plans for the day.

Still, I often thought about Rosanna. Where had she ended up going? Was she okay? What was she doing now? Did she hate me? I wouldn't blame her if she did after the way I'd acted. I spent so much time ruminating with regret.

"Your scar looks better," my mother said one morning as she assessed my face. "It must be healing."

"It's not healing." I scowled. "It's a scar. A permanent part of my face."

She nodded. "I think it looks better."

"That's because you're my mom. Probably wishful thinking. I see it every day. I know how hideous it looks."

"No." She shook her head. "You're still so handsome."

I resisted rolling my eyes. "You're saying that because you're my mother."

Family dinners were the loud, happy times I remembered. My mom and sister filled me in with all the happenings with relatives, which cousin was where, doing what, and so on.

"It's better this way. I get to hear the updates but don't have to sit through the conversations," I teased.

My father chuckled.

My mom swatted my arm. "This is family we're talking about.

I grinned at her. "And I'm here with my family."

I gazed at my parents. They'd been married for thirty years now. Although they bickered often, I saw the love. The way she would make sure he ate healthy despite his sweet tooth. That way he'd ensure her car was safe to drive. The way they took care of each other. I longed for something like it. Rosanna and I had taken care of each other during that short time we'd been together. Was I a fool to throw something so special away?

Too late now.

One day, my sister walked up to me in the family room. "Game?"

"Sure."

"How about Monopoly?"

"Definitely not." Not so soon after that moment with Rosanna and how hot things had turned. We'd ended up all over each other that night, abandoning the game. Would I ever look at a game of Monopoly the same way again?

"Why not?"

"It takes too long," I replied.

"Are you going somewhere anytime soon?" She motioned to the front door.

"Nope." I shook my head. "How about Rummy?"

"Fine."

While we played cards, I asked her, "What's new in your life?"

She filled me in on her activities, classes, and so on. "Rummy!" she declared as she reaped the benefit from my distraction.

Her competitive streak reminded me of Rosanna's. She was so sweet until we pulled out a board game, but then turned ruthless.

No, I couldn't have every little thing remind me of her. I came here to get away from the memories in my cottage, but now she was haunting me here.

Would I ever be able to forget her?

ONE DAY PASSED INTO THE NEXT, AND I STILL THOUGHT ABOUT Rosanna. By the time I prepared to go back to Vermont a few days later, I'd declared myself a full-blown idiot.

I dwelled on every mistake I'd made with her, from pulling away after the ski trip to deleting her document and then kicking her out. I'd acted like a full-out beast.

Now all I could so was simmer in guilt and regret.

Could I blame her for worrying about what was going on? After all, I'd shut her out. If I was in her position, would I have done the same thing?

Possibly.

No, probably.

That made me a grade-A hypocrite.

We had something special. As soon as our relationship had started to bloom, I'd destroyed it. I'd crushed it as easy as squeezing flower petals in my hand and then sending them crashing to the floor.

She'd wanted to talk. I refused. Why?

Because I was vulnerable? Afraid?

Both? Likely.

Deep down, I acted out of fear. I rejected her before she could reject me.

WHEN I RETURNED TO THE COTTAGE, THE EMPTINESS ALMOST swallowed me. No longer did it have the delicious aromas of whatever Rosanna was cooking to greet me. No longer did it have her warm me with a smile when I walked into the room. No longer did it have the sound of her beautiful voice as she talked to me or hummed or sang.

Even the temperature was cold. We'd often heated the cottage with a fire. The absence in the hearth was exacerbated by the cold stone walls surrounding me.

I was alone.

That had been the plan when I'd isolated myself here, but after those weeks with Rosanna, acute loneliness pierced my soul. I missed her.

Still, there was nothing I could do about it now. After the way I'd treated her, she'd never want to speak to me again. I screwed up badly. She was moving on. So should I.

Two more days passed without any respite. I avoided the cottage as much as possible and spent the time hiking the woods or cross-country skiing if the weather wasn't too harsh. I wouldn't return until hunger, fatigue, or the cold drove me back to face the empty space.

When I brought in the mail the next afternoon, there was a letter. My name and address were handwritten, and the return address was from R. Carreiro. My heart thumped against my ribs. Rosanna.

Wait, what if this was a bad thing? She was reaming me out for being such a jerk. I dropped the letter on the table and leapt away, then stared at it from several feet away.

Dozens of possibilities of what could be inside crashed in

my head, most of them fearing the worst. She hated me now and wanted to let me know exactly how she felt.

I deserved that.

Pacing before the letter, I debated my options. I could toss it in the fire and avoid the scathing words that were sure to add more torment to my anguished soul.

Or I could man up and open the damn thing.

At least it would put an end to my speculation. I approached the table with slow steps and picked up the envelope. My heart raced as I opened it with trembling fingers. I pulled out the letter and took a deep breath to brace myself for the reprimand.

Then I started to read it.

Dear Leo,

I'm so sorry about what happened the day I left. It was wrong of me to invade your space, especially after I'd promised not to do so.

Once you started to pull away after the ski trip, it became clear you weren't over your ex. You were in dark moods and withdrawn and spent more and more time in your studio. I wasn't sure if it was to avoid me specifically or the world in general. I worried about you— and then feared the worst. I had to make sure you were okay.

I know this is supposed to be an apology letter, but I don't regret ensuring that you were safe. Because if I could have done something and didn't, I'd never forgive myself. But I am truly sorry to have ever caused you pain.

If you fear that others will judge you for your art, don't. You're an artist. You've chosen a way to express your pain in a positive way. I admire that. While I do so with words, you do so with your paintbrush. And you created such magnificent paintings. Yes, some are raw and violent, and maybe it makes you feel vulnerable, but they are real. *They're created by someone who's experienced so much; something many of us might never comprehend. Art isn't always pretty, but it can bring comfort or insight to a dark world.*

I understand why you're disturbed that I wrote about you in that document. I don't know if this will bring you any ease, but it was just a freewriting exercise. Nobody would have ever seen it but me.

I wasn't spying on you for your mother or my own gain. I didn't mean to exploit you, but maybe you're right and I did so unintentionally. There are so many things I admire about you, from your courage to your independence, your considerate side to your artistic talent, and I just wanted to capture some of those traits as I brainstormed ideas. I promise I wasn't writing about you or sharing your story. I would never do that without your consent.

Anyway, I know you don't want to hear from me. I am truly sorry for any pain I caused. I wish you all the happiness and hope you can someday forgive me.

LOVE,
Rosanna

I STARED AT THE LETTER FOR A FULL MINUTE BEFORE READING IT again. I'd been a jerk, and yet, she apologized, taking some responsibility. She was a much better person than I could ever be.

And then there were the final two words: Love, Rosanna.

After the horrible way I'd treated her, she'd still signed off with that sentiment. I ran my fingertip over those two words. Then I lifted the handwritten letter to my nose and inhaled as if I could scent her on the stationery.

I didn't know how to process her words. The biggest takeaway was that she didn't hate me and curse me out for being a jerk.

When I went to bed that night, I placed the letter under the pillow. It didn't make up for the fact that my bed was cold and empty without her there, but in a strange way, it brought me comfort. I should try to understand her perspective more. Rosanna had her reasons for doing what she did and much of it was in reaction to my behavior. She was right. I had pulled away after the ski trip, but not for the reasons that she suspected. And I was anxious to show my art to the world for fear of being judged.

By the morning, I'd made up my mind. I needed to talk to someone to control my anger so I wouldn't explode like that again.

Most of all, I needed to go to Rosanna and talk to her. Tell her how I really feel. Keeping things inside didn't help anyone.

I had her address. It was time to take a road trip to Boston.

ONCE I STARTED THE DRIVE, COUNTLESS DOUBTS POKED AT MY resolve. She might not want to see me. That was a goodbye letter. The back of my neck prickled.

That was fear talking again. If she had the nerve to bare herself and apologize in that letter, I could have the balls to walk up to her rather than hiding away like I had been doing since my medical discharge.

She could reject me, yes. It would hurt like hell, but at least I'd know. And that was better than spending the rest of my life wondering if things could have been different if I'd taken a chance.

I flipped through songs on the radio and stopped on a familiar song—Toto's "Rosanna." Whereas the last time I'd heard it, I'd thrown the speaker, this time the song soothed me. As I drove through a small Vermont town, I stopped by a bookstore. Rosanna loved to read. I wanted to get her a gift to go with my apology.

Once my purchase was packaged up, I continued the drive south.

When I reached her apartment, it was afternoon. I rang the

bell to her apartment. A young woman with brown hair pulled into a ponytail and college sweatshirt answered and said Rosanna wasn't home.

"Do you know where she is?" I asked.

"Who are you?" she questioned.

I didn't blame her for asking. "A friend of Rosanna's." If I was even that. I hoped I was more than a friend to Rosanna, but I wouldn't push it. "My name is Leo. She spent time with me in Vermont over break."

Recognition widened the woman's eyes. "Oh, I heard about you." She tilted her head. "She's on campus."

"Do you know where I can find her?"

Her roommate gave me some ideas of where Rosanna could be on campus. It looked like my next step was scouring the grounds in the hopes of seeing her.

It wasn't easy.

I treaded back and forth through the old stone and brick buildings, hoping for a sign of her in between classes. Since I had her number, I could have texted her, but it was better to talk to her face to face. At least, she couldn't misread my meaning through a message.

Late afternoon, I spotted her in the student union. Rosanna sat at a table. A strange fluttering spread in my chest, and my breath quickened. She sat across from a man who I recognized as the guy she'd spoken to on a video chat at the cottage.

Needles stabbed my spine. I forced myself to shove my speculation aside. She'd said he was just a friend, and I should believe her. Not let my imagination run wild as it did before, contemplating whether there were any benefits to their friendship.

What I'd learned was that there was so much I didn't know. I'd assumed and had been utterly wrong. She deserved a chance to be heard. I'd shut her down back in Vermont, and it had been a mistake.

My biggest mistake thus far. I swallowed. Would it be one I could recover from?

My heartbeat echoed in my ears. My palms heated, and I wiped them on the sides of my pants. Within seconds, I'd know my answer to the question that tormented me.

Would she give me a chance?

She might think I was an uber creep to come find her here at her college. Or even a stalker.

Stop making assumptions.

Right.

I pushed myself to take one step after the other, reducing the distance between us. My heart galloped up to my throat. Pretty boy looked up at me as I approached.

I ignored him to focus on her. "Rosanna, can we talk?"

CHAPTER 17

ROSANNA

*L*eo was here? So many emotions danced inside me, I didn't know what I was feeling. My mouth fell open, and my hand fluttered to my chest.

After gaping at him, I finally found words. "Leo, what are you doing here?"

"To see you." He adjusted his stance as if nervous. "And apologize."

Daniel stood. "I need to go." He gave me a knowing look before nodding to Leo and motioning to his empty seat. "Here, you can have my seat."

After gaping, I finally snapped out of it and introduced them both.

They exchanged greetings, and then Daniel walked away.

Leo turned to me. "Do you mind if I sit for a minute?"

"No." I motioned to the empty chair. "Please."

Once he sat, he asked, "Are you dating him?"

"Daniel?" My brows arched. "The guy who was sitting here."

"Yes." Leo's mouth was a hard line but otherwise unreadable.

"No." With a grin, I added, "His boyfriend Marcus might be a little pissed off."

Leo blinked at me. "Boyfriend?"

"Yes. We're just friends."

He rubbed the back of his neck and stared at the sidewalk. "I'm sorry. About everything. I acted like a downright beast. Deleting your work was inexcusable. I was afraid and lashed out." He heaved forward with a weighted exhale. "I pushed you away and have been regretting it ever since."

"I'm sorry, too. I shouldn't have gone into your studio." I leaned back in my chair and ran my hand through my hair. "I shouldn't have used you as inspiration for my writing exercises."

Leo gave me a somber nod. "You explained in your letter."

"I swear I was just brainstorming, coming up with traits for characters," I babbled, repeating what I'd already wrote. "There were many things about you I admired and found fascinating." Then I shook my head. "But I never would have written about you without your consent."

"I should've let you explain rather than react so maliciously and destroy your work." His gaze rose to meet mine. "I know I shut you out, and I regret it. I understand why you'd think I wasn't over Eva after the way I'd reacted. It wasn't because I'm not over her." He drummed his fingers on the table. "It was a reminder of why I wasn't right for a relationship, not then, and especially not now. I didn't think I was good for you. I thought you'd want more. You *deserved* more. Better." His gaze filled with warmth. "But with you, everything changed. You accepted me as I am. You didn't want the things I could give you; you wanted *me*. You made me feel whole. Capable of being in a relationship with someone I love." He reached across the table and brushed his fingers against mine. "That is, if I haven't ruined everything."

My heart fluttered. Love? Did Leo love me?

There was so much that had been left unsaid between us. Now was the chance to fix that. "Leo, I think we both faced some triggers then. I want to tell you something I've never told anyone. I'm not using it as an excuse or to justify breaking my promise and your trust, but I think you should know as it was a devastating period in my life, and it still affects me to this day."

"You can tell me anything," he said.

I glanced down at the table. "After my mother died, my father told me it was an accident. That she took too many sleeping pills. I don't think that was the truth. I think he was shielding me from what really happened, especially as I was so young. I think it was intentional." My voice croaked on the last word.

"Oh, Rosanna." His voice was gentle. "I'm so sorry."

"I know she loved us, but she was often distant and sad. I didn't really understand what was going on back then. The older I've gotten, and the more I've learned about similar stories, the more it confirms what I suspect."

"You've never talked to your father about this?"

I shook my head. "No. It would bring him more pain and won't bring my mother back." She brought her fingers together, clasping her hands. "Once you started withdrawing, I started to worry. And thinking about how your mother didn't want you alone over the holidays... And then my concerns escalated as I feared the worse could happen. Maybe I wasn't thinking straight, letting my past cloud my better judgment. Maybe I was just too nosy and desperate to know what you were keeping hidden from me. Possibly both. I'm not trying to excuse my actions. I should've talked to you first. I shouldn't have broken your trust."

"Oh hell, I'm sorry, Rosanna. I never should have put you through that." He leaned forward and took my hand. "And I never should have lashed out at you like that. I made an appointment to talk to a therapist because I never want to yell at you like that again. If you give me another chance, I promise to be more open with you."

What exactly did he mean by that?

He pulled his hand away and reached down into a shopping bag that he'd put beside him on the sidewalk. He pulled out a gift wrapped in shiny red paper with a silver bow and handed it to me across the table.

"What's this?" I asked.

"A late Christmas present. I saw this, and it was meant for you." His mouth curled into a grin. "Besides, it helps with my groveling." He motioned to the present. "Open it."

After I tore off the paper, I stared at a beautiful leather-bound edition of *Beauty and the Beast.* "What's this?"

"You see, this is called a book. It can be both a noun and a verb, my creative writing major," he explained in that same teasing way he did when explaining a shovel back at his stone cottage. "In this case, it's a noun."

I groaned. "I know what a book is, Leo. Why are you giving it to me?"

He closed his eyes. "I'm being an idiot again." He exhaled with a heavy whoosh. "Because what I'm doing makes me feel vulnerable. I never feel more exposed as when I'm around you." He reopened his eyes and gazed at me with warmth. "And you're the only one I want to open up to in this way."

I gaped at him. Was I really hearing this?

"The thing is, Rosanna, I'm in love with you. I fell in love with you but was too stubborn and scared to admit it."

"You love me?" I repeated, gaping at him.

"Yes." He pointed at the book in my hand. "I know I've been a beast, and you've been my beauty, inside and out. This book is the first to go in your library."

"My *what?*"

He slanted his head and gave me an amused gaze. "Do I need to explain what a library is?"

I tried not to smile but couldn't help it. "Of course not."

"Good. Because I want you to have a library and study where you can write. You can take the empty room in the cottage. Or we can go anywhere else, and you can create one there. I don't care where we go. I only want to be with you—if you feel the same about me."

I couldn't be hearing this correctly. "Let me get this straight. You want to be with me. And you want to build me a library?"

"Yes. With a study for you to write or however you'd like to use it."

"In your cottage?"

"Sure." He shrugged. "There's plenty of room."

My fingers fluttered to my lips. "You want me to move in with you?"

"Yes." He took my hands. "Whenever you'd like. I know you're here finishing school. I'll move down here. Or I'll wait for you in the cottage if you want to come there. I don't care where I go or how long it takes, I'll do whatever I have to, Rosanna. Because you're the one. And I love you."

My eyes watered. "Oh, Leo." I stood and rushed around the table to him. When he rose, I threw my arms around his neck and hugged him. "I love you, too."

People around us stared, but I didn't care.

He laughed. When we pulled apart, he gazed at me, delight in his blue eyes. "Do you need time to think about it?"

My insides were thumping on overdrive as I replayed his words in my head. One emotion morphed into another since I'd spotted him. But now I was with Leo, and I was happy.

Slanting my head, I smiled. "I found writing in the cottage quite inspiring. It's much better to work on my final project there rather than being distracted by all that's going on in the city."

"Is it now?" His brows arched.

"Yes. I was very happy there."

"As was I with you there."

"I can write from anywhere. I want to go back to the cottage with you."

His smile stretched from one end of campus to the other. "Yes. Let's go home."

"Home," I repeated. The perfect place to be with the one you loved.

As we walked through the campus, he took my hand. People passing from the other direction glanced at him, their gazes immediately darting to his scar. I knew putting himself out here in such a public place was difficult for him. No, not just difficult, downright excruciating. Emotions rose, and tears pooled in my eyes. My reclusive SEAL had come all this way and was willing to endure the stares for me?

He turned to me, appearing to ignore the public scrutiny. "First, I asked you to stay the night. Then, I asked you to stay the weekend. Later, I asked you to stay for the holidays." His blue eyes widened with vulnerability. "Now I'm asking you to stay."

I arched one brow. "For how long this time?"

"For as long as you can put up with a grump like me." He slanted a smile. "I'm hoping forever."

My heart pounded with jubilation. I couldn't believe what I was hearing. "Leo." I placed my hand over my chest. "I'm in shock. I don't know what to say."

"You don't have to say anything yet," he replied, caressing my palm. "I know you have to finish out your final semester, and I'd never do anything to jeopardize what you've worked so hard to accomplish. You do what's best for you."

Giddiness almost answered for me, but I had to think of the practicalities. "I can finish up my final semester remotely as long as I have a Wi-Fi connection."

"Ah ha," he teased and raised his index finger. "I know someplace that has that—the cottage."

"Looks like I should give it a go. Let's give it a try." I cupped his cheeks and leaned up to kiss him. "Let's give *us* a try."

LEO

"I listened to your song driving down," I told Rosanna as I played it on the ride back.

"Oh?" Her eyes gleamed with delight.

"It tormented me in a way," I admitted. "I missed you. Wanted to be with you."

She reached over and squeezed my thigh. "I'm with you now."

"Yes." I shook my head. "I'm not going to be an idiot and let you get away again."

She laughed. "Sounds like a good plan."

We had plenty of time to talk on the three-plus-hour drive through Massachusetts and into Vermont. Rosanna told me how she'd spent some time at Daniel's house after she left the cottage and then found some roommates who were subletting a room for the spring. Her next task was looking for a job.

"Don't worry about that now," I said. "I'll pay the rent for the rest of the semester."

"You don't have to do that."

"Please. It's the least I can do. If I hadn't pushed you away, things might have gone differently."

"How about you?" she asked. "What have you done since I left?"

"I went to visit my family."

"You did?" Her eyes widened with happiness.

"Yes, it was about time. Plus"—I exhaled with a weary sigh —"the cottage had too many memories of you. Being there without you hurt."

"I'm glad I'm going back with you." Her gentle eyes warmed me.

"Me too."

Once we arrived, we walked to the front door of the cottage.

"Welcome home," she said.

She stared at the door. "How funny. The first time I arrived I was somewhat nervous about what I'd face inside." She turned to me. "Now it's home, most of all because of the man who lives there who I love."

My heart thumped. "You love me?"

"Of course. I love you, Leo."

"And I love you." I bent down to kiss her. After we pulled apart, I opened the door.

Rosanna didn't have many belongings to bring inside, but we carried the bags and boxes into the living room. Just seeing them stacked up there brought me comfort. The cottage had been so empty without her. I'd be happy with her filling every nook of every corner with her possessions, a reminder that she was here.

"Where should we put these?" she asked.

I glanced up at the stairs, picturing her temporary bedroom. The last time I was in there with her, I'd been such a beast, destroying her work.

"We'll figure it out," I said. "As long as you sleep in the bed with me."

She nodded. "Deal." She pulled the book I'd given her out of the bag. "First things first. This needs to go in its proper home."

"After you." I bowed and welcomed her to proceed.

She climbed up the stairs, and I followed.

When I glanced down the hall at my studio, I said, "One thing." I walked down the hall and opened the door. It felt odd to expose my work that made me feel so vulnerable, but I vowed not to be closed off any longer, so I wouldn't push her away again. "No more secrets. You can enter whenever you'd like. You can ask me whatever you want."

She gazed at me with understanding. "We have plenty of time to share."

"True." I pointed at the book in her hand. "So where are you going to put it?"

She cocked her head. "I believe someone promised me a library." She headed into the room that was being used for storage and circled around. "I think it will be just beautiful in here." She put the book on a small, three-tier bookshelf that was covered with odds and ends right now.

I motioned to each wall. "This is your canvas."

When I pictured her writing here in her library, it reminded me of the work I'd destroyed. "Rosanna, one thing."

"What is it?"

I gulped. "You can use whatever you'd like of my story for your book."

Her eyes gleamed with emotion. "I don't need to do that, Leo. And I don't want to share you with anyone." She leaned up on her tiptoes to kiss me. "You're already the hero of my story."

EPILOGUE

ROSANNA

"Merry Christmas." Leo woke me up with a kiss on the forehead and the steaming mug of tea with milk.

"Merry Christmas." I sat up and took a sip of the tea from the mug he offered me. I took another sip. "I hope you're hungry for apple cinnamon pancakes."

"Absolutely," he agreed. "We have to celebrate your family's tradition." He rubbed his stomach.

Half-an-hour later, we sat at the dining room table eating our pancakes. The scent of baked apples and cinnamon filled the room, my family's tradition. A Christmas tree that we'd picked out was decorated with ornaments both of Leo's childhood and mine as well as the pine cone ones we'd made for each other last Christmas.

Holiday music played. Leo had created a playlist that didn't include any Elvis songs so as not to take me by surprise. I'd had time to myself yesterday and had listened to songs that reminded me of my mother yesterday. I'd talked to her out loud, telling her how things were better for me now than ever. I'd graduated while both Leo and my father watched from the stands. Since then, I'd picked up some freelance writing gigs. I'd even sent my manuscript that I'd worked on for my final project to an editor to see how I could improve it if I decided to self-publish it one day. It needed some work, but it was in much better shape than I thought.

Leo put his fork down on his empty plate. "You sure know the way to my heart is through my stomach." He grinned. He'd used that line several times since he'd done so on my first day in the cottage when he'd warned me not to try to win him over that way.

"That was my plan to get you from the beginning," I replied with my often-used retort and smiled.

"I want to give you a present." He gestured for me to follow him to the Christmas tree and pulled out a long, skinny package wrapped in red and green plaid paper. It was about as tall as him.

"I wonder what this could be," I joked. The shape of the present gave me a clue since he'd spoken of how I needed my own pair this winter.

"It's a great mystery," he replied with a wink.

I opened the package, and it was what I suspected—cross-country skis. They were bright red. "Ooh, I love them. The color is festive." I glanced at him. "Maybe I'll be better on these."

"You did great with my sister's old pair." He walked over to the window. "I thought cross country skiing could be one of our traditions. After all, it is a white Christmas."

It was indeed. The snowy forests and mountains were covered with white. I loved living here in the mountains. Yes, it was remote, and the winter could be harsh, but there were so many things I loved about living here in nature, so different from the bustle in the city.

Besides, I could warm up with Leo here in the cottage.

Also, it was the perfect place for me to write. After I moved back here with Leo in January, I'd started to set up the room next to mine. It was now a library with built-in bookshelves and a walnut desk area I'd found at an antique store a few towns away. I set it up to look over the mountains in the distance when I wrote. The picturesque view with the vast open space often gave me free rein to let my imagination run free.

"I think skiing after all those pancakes is a great idea," I agreed. "After all, we're going to spend the day eating and drinking."

Leo arched one brow. "I know some other ways we can burn off those calories."

"You're ready to go again so soon after last night? We'd stayed up late making love in front of the fireplace. I'd surprised him with a bearskin rug that I thought was the perfect touch for the cabin.

"With you, I'm always raring to go." He cupped my cheek and kissed me. "Wait, I see one more thing." He walked over to the tree and pulled out a small, red velvet box that was tucked back in the branches.

I sucked in a breath.

Leo returned to me and bent down on one knee. "Meeting you was the best thing that ever happened to me, Rosanna." His mouth slanted into a grin. "I guess I have to thank my mother one day for that. But today is about you and me."

I opened my mouth to say something, but nothing came out.

He opened the box and presented a gorgeous round diamond on a rose gold band. "Will you marry me?"

LEO

On one knee, I awaited the answer to the most important question I'd ever asked. Rosanna stared at me, eyes glistening and lower lip trembling.

Uh oh, had I made a mistake?

Her mouth spread into a luminous smile that reached her eyes. "Of course I'll marry you, Leo!"

She leapt out of the seat, and I stood. I spread my arms wide, and she fell against me.

"You will?" I wrapped my arms around her as if capturing this moment and hoping it wasn't all a dream.

"Yes." She pulled her head back a few inches and gazed up at me. "I love you. There's no place I'd rather be, and no one else I'd rather be with."

I gazed down at her, the woman I cherished and loved. In her eyes, I saw love and acceptance and understanding, all the things I never knew I needed until I met her. I tipped her chin up. "Merry Christmas." Then I bent down and kissed her.

I held her close as we kissed in front of the Christmas tree. When we pulled apart, both of us were slightly breathless.

She beamed at me. "The merriest one yet."

THE DAY AFTER CHRISTMAS, WE STARTED OUR TRIP TO VISIT family. First, we were driving to my parents' house in New York. After a couple of nights there, we were flying to North Carolina to visit her family. We'd each met the other's family during the summer.

When we reached my parents' house, my mother ran out the front door to greet us. We hadn't told her the news about the engagement yet, but her gaze darted down to Rosanna's hand, and she squealed.

"Is it? Are you?"

"Yes, we're engaged," I confirmed with a smile.

My mother bear hugged us both. "Oh, I'm so happy! Tell me everything. Wait. Let's go inside."

Once we went into the house and took off our coats, we sat in the living room with my father and sister. I told them how I'd proposed on Christmas morning.

My mother practically tackled Rosanna in another hug. "I'm so glad you're going to be my daughter."

"And I finally have a sister!" Tia declared.

Tia and Rosanna had clicked right away. Rosanna was only two years older, and Tia had just started grad school, so they found plenty to talk about. My mother, of course, loved Rosanna instantly and thanked her for "taking care of her boy." Even though I was almost thirty, I'd always be her boy.

"Mom, I know this is overdue," I said, "but thank you for bringing Rosanna into my life."

My mother brushed it aside. "I'm just glad to see you happy."

"More than I ever imagined possible." I gazed at my future wife and smiled.

ROSANNA

After a few days with Leo's family, we visited mine and shared the news about our engagement. My stepsisters were more interested in the ring and talked about what they'd wear to the wedding. I just grinned and exchanged a look with Leo. Visits were more tolerable with him around.

My father was overjoyed. He pulled me aside. "I'm glad you found a good man."

"The best," I replied.

We spent a couple more days there and then returned home.

"Home sweet home," I declared once I stepped inside the

cottage.

"We survived family holiday madness," Leo added with a laugh. "My family loves you, of course. How could they not? I'm sure everyone does the moment they meet you."

I laughed and slanted a gaze at him. "I seem to remember somebody pushing me out the door in this cottage when he first met me."

"Sounds like a grouch," he replied with a sly grin.

"Oh, he was indeed." I flashed a knowing smile at him. "But he has a soft spot inside."

Leo fixed his gaze on me. "Only for you, Rosanna." He leaned over and kissed me. "Only for you."

A Note from the Author:

Thanks for reading Leo and Rosanna's romance. I hope you enjoyed visiting Vermont in the winter with them. Their romance is a standalone story in the Anchor Me series with second chances, suspense, fake relationships, or friends to lovers romance. Escape to a Newport wedding or a tropical island with Navy SEALs, Marines, and Veterans—and even a few fur babies!

Binge the series with brothers Angelo, Vince, Matty, and more.

Download Antonio, a second chance with a Marine novella as a welcome gift when you subscribe to my newsletter at lisacarlislebooks.com.

Happy reading!

~ Lisa

GO BEHIND THE SCENES

Want more from the stories? Want to be the first to read new books before they're released?

Join me at Patreon to go behind the scenes with exclusive content, bonus scenes and stories from the Anchor Me series, and signed books.

https://www.patreon.com/lisacarlisle

BE A VIP READER!

Join my Facebook reader group!
Visit lisacarlislebooks.com to subscribe to my reader news-letter and see the latest releases. New readers receive a welcome gift, exclusive bonus content and free books including Antonio's story.

ACKNOWLEDGMENTS

Here's a shout out to the team! It takes a lot of time and effort to move from the strange, random ideas to my head to a complete story. Thank you to all the people who are part of this publishing journey, including my critique group, editors, cover artists, beta readers, ARC readers, and Street Team!

And thank you to my family for their support and patience while I'm in another world, working on my stories.

Lisa

ABOUT THE AUTHOR

USA Today bestselling author Lisa Carlisle loves stories with misfits or outcasts. Her romances have been named Top Picks at Night Owl Reviews and the Romance Reviews.

When she was younger, she worked in a variety of jobs, moving to various countries. She served in the military in Okinawa, Japan; backpacked alone through Europe; and worked in Paris before returning to the U.S. She owned a bookstore for a few years as she loves to read. She's now married to a fantastic man, and they have two kids and two crazy cats.

Visit her website at:
Lisacarlislebooks.com

Sign up for her newsletter to hear about new releases, specials, and freebies:
http://lisacarlislebooks.com/subscribe/

Lisa loves to connect with readers. You can find her on:

Facebook
  TikTok
  Instagram
  Pinterest
  Goodreads

BOOK LIST

Visit LisaCarlisleBooks.com to learn more!

Anchor Me

Second chances, suspense, fake relationships, or friends to lovers romance. Escape to a Newport wedding or a tropical island with Navy SEALs, Marines, and Veterans—and even a few fur babies!

All feature a different hero and can be read as standalone.

- *Antonio (a novella available as a welcome gift to new subscribers at lisacarlislebooks.com)*
- *Angelo*
- *Vince*
- *Matty*
- *Jack*
- *Slade*
- *Mark*
- *Leo*

Night Eagle Operations

A paranormal romantic suspense novel

- *When Darkness Whispers*

Salem Supernaturals

Paranormal chick lit with comedy, romance, and mystery!

- *Rebel Spell*
- *Hot in Witch City*
- *Dancing with My Elf*

- *Night Wedding*
- *Bite Wedding*
- *Sprite Wedding*

White Mountain Shifters (A Wolf Shifter Trilogy)

Howls Romance

When three wolf shifters meet their fated mates at their ski resort, the forbidden attraction may spark a war.

- *The Reluctant Wolf and His Fated Mate*
- *The Wolf and His Forbidden Witch*
- *The Alpha and His Enemy Wolf*

The White Mountain Shifters series is connected to the Salem Supernaturals and Underground Encounters series.

Underground Encounters

Steamy paranormal romances set in an underground goth club that attracts vampires, witches, shifters, and gargoyles.

- *Book 0: CURSED (a gargoyle shifter story)*
- *Book 1: SMOLDER (a vampire / firefighter romance)*
- *Book 2: FIRE (a witch / firefighter romance)*
- *Book 3: IGNITE (a feline shifter / rock star romance)*
- *Book 4: BURN (a vampire / shapeshifter rock romance)*
- *Book 5: HEAT (a gargoyle shifter romance)*
- *Book 6: BLAZE (a gargoyle shifter rockstar romance)*
- *Book 7: COMBUST (vampire / witch romances)*
- *Book 8: INFLAME (a gargoyle shifter / witch romance)*
- *Book 9: TORCH (a gargoyle shifter / werewolf romance)*
- *Book 10: SCORCH (an incubus vs succubus demon romance)*

Stone Sentries Trilogy

Meet your perfect match the night of the super moon — or your perfect match for the night. A cop teams up with a gargoyle shifter when demons attack Boston.

- *Tempted by the Gargoyle*
- *Enticed by the Gargoyle*
- *Captivated by the Gargoyle*

Highland Gargoyles (A Complete Series)

When a witch sneaks into forbidden territory on a divided isle, she's caught by a shifter. One risk changes the fate for all...

- *Knights of Stone: Mason*
- *Knights of Stone: Lachlan*
- *Knights of Stone: Bryce*
- *Seth: a wolf shifter romance*
- *Knights of Stone: Calum*
- *Stone Cursed*
- *Knights of Stone: Gavin*

Chateau Seductions

An art colony on a remote New England island lures creative types— and supernatural characters. Steamy paranormal romances.

- *Darkness Rising*
- *Dark Velvet*
- *Dark Muse*
- *Dark Stranger*
- *Dark Pursuit*

Berkano Vampires

A shared author world with dystopian paranormal romances.

- *Immortal Resistance*

Blood Courtesans

A shared author world with the vampire blood courtesans.

- *Pursued: Mia*

Visit LisaCarlisleBooks.com to learn more!

Printed in Great Britain
by Amazon

15726380R00114